The Adventures of
PINOCCHIO
Carlo Collodi & Roberto Innocenti

The Adventures of
PINOCCHIO
Carlo Collodi & Roberto Innocenti

DESIGNED BY RITA MARSHALL

A TOM MASCHLER BOOK

JONATHAN CAPE • LONDON

THE ADVENTURES OF PINOCCHIO
A JONATHAN CAPE BOOK 0 224 07056 8

Published in Great Britain by Jonathan Cape,
an imprint of Random House Children's Books.
This edition first published by Creative Editions, an imprint of
The Creative Company, 123 South Broad Street,
Mankato MN 56001 USA

First Jonathan Cape edition published 1988
This edition published 2005

1 3 5 7 9 10 8 6 4 2

Illustrations copyright © Roberto Innocenti, 2005
Text based on a translation by Mary Alice Murray
Designed by Rita Marshall

Le Avventure di Pinocchio by Carlo Collodi was first published in Italy in 1882

RANDOM HOUSE CHILDREN'S BOOKS
61–63 Uxbridge Road, London W5 5SA
A division of The Random House Group Ltd

RANDOM HOUSE AUSTRALIA (PTY) LTD
20 Alfred Street, Milsons Point, Sydney,
New South Wales 2061, Australia

RANDOM HOUSE NEW ZEALAND LTD
18 Poland Road, Glenfield, Auckland 10, New Zealand

RANDOM HOUSE (PTY) LTD
Endulini, 5A Jubilee Road, Parktown 2193, South Africa

THE RANDOM HOUSE GROUP Limited Reg. No. 954009
www.kidsatrandomhouse.co.uk

A CIP catalogue record for this book is available from the British Library.

Printed in China

To Carlo Collodi and
my daughter Alessandra

Other books illustrated by Roberto Innocenti

Rose Blanche

Written by Ian McEwan

Nutcracker

Written by E. T. A. Hoffmann

The Last Resort

Written by J. Patrick Lewis

Erika's Story

Written by Ruth Vander Zee

The Adventures of
PINOCCHIO
Carlo Collodi & Roberto Innocenti

{ Chapter 1 }

Master Cherry finds a strange piece of wood

nce upon a time there was . . .

"A king!" you will say.

But you are wrong. Once upon a time there was a piece of wood.

This wood was not valuable; it was a common log just like those that are used for firewood in the winter.

I cannot say how, but one day this piece of wood was found in the shop of an old carpenter called Master Antonio. But everybody called him Master Cherry because the end of his nose was always as red and shiny as a ripe cherry.

As soon as Master Cherry spotted the wood he beamed with delight and rubbing his hands together with satisfaction, he said, "This has come at just the right time — it will make the perfect leg for a little table."

Having said this, he picked up an axe to remove the bark and the rough surface with. But just as he was about to start, he heard a very small voice say, "Don't hit me!"

Master Cherry was astonished.

He looked around the room, terrified, to see whether he could see where the voice had come from, but there was nobody there! He looked under the bench — nobody; he looked into a cupboard that was always shut — nobody; he looked into a basket of wood shavings and sawdust — nobody; he even opened the door of the shop and

glanced into the street — and still nobody. But who could it be?

"I see," he said, laughing and scratching his wig. "The voice must have been my imagination."

He picked up the axe again and hit the piece of wood hard.

"Oh! Oh! Ouch!" cried the same little voice.

This time Master Cherry was petrified. His eyes and mouth widened with fright, and his tongue hung right out of his mouth. As soon as he could speak again, but still stuttering and trembling with fear, he said, "But where on Earth can that little voice have come from? There's definitely nobody. Surely this piece of wood cannot cry like a child. I can't believe it. This piece of wood is just a log for fuel like all the others and it would only burn long enough to boil a pan of beans. So how can anyone be hidden inside it? And if anyone is inside, he will be in trouble. I'll show him!"

Master Cherry grabbed the piece of wood and started mercilessly beating it against the wall.

He stopped to listen for the little voice. He waited two minutes – nothing; five minutes – nothing; ten minutes – still nothing.

"I see," he said again, forcing himself to laugh as he adjusted his wig. "The little voice must have just been my imagination," he said as he started again.

But by this time, Master Cherry was quite frightened, so he tried to sing to give himself courage.

He put the axe down and picked up his plane to smooth and polish the wood. But as he ran it up and down, he heard the same little voice and this time it was laughing, "Stop it! You're tickling me!"

Poor Master Cherry fell down as if he had been struck by lightning and when he opened his eyes he realized he was lying on the floor.

His face was quite different. Even the end of his nose, instead of being bright red, as it usually was, had become blue from fright.

{ Chapter 2 }

Geppetto makes a wonderful puppet

t that moment, someone knocked on the door.

"Come in," said Master Cherry, too weak to get up.

A lively little old man walked into the shop. His name was Geppetto but all the local boys called him "Polendina," because his yellow wig looked just like the Indian corn pudding, polendina. It made Geppetto furious whenever he heard it.

"Good day, Master Antonio," said Geppetto. "What are you doing on the floor?"

"I am teaching the ants to read."

"I hope it does you good!"

"What brings you here, Geppetto?"

"My legs of course. But I have also come to ask you a favour."

"At your service," replied the carpenter, rising to his knees.

"This morning I had an idea."

"Let's hear it then."

"I thought I would make a beautiful wooden puppet — a wonderful dancing, singing puppet that could do tricks and acrobatics. With this puppet I would travel the world and earn my living. What do you think?"

"Well done, Polendina!" exclaimed the same little voice. But it was impossible to

say where it came from.

Hearing himself called Polendina, Geppetto became red with rage, and turning to the carpenter, he said furiously, "Why did you call me that?"

"Call you what?"

"You called me Polendina!"

"I did not."

"Are you saying I called myself Polendina? It was you, I say!"

"No!"

"Yes!"

"No!"

"Yes!"

They became more and more angry and started fighting. They flew at each other, biting and scratching.

When the fight was over, Master Antonio had Geppetto's yellow wig in his hand and Geppetto realized that the carpenter's grey wig was clenched between his teeth.

"Give me back my wig," shouted Master Antonio.

"Give me back mine too, and then let's say sorry."

The two old men, now with their own wigs back, shook hands and swore that they would always be friends.

"Well, then, Geppetto," said the carpenter, to prove that there were no hard feelings, "what is the favour you wanted to ask me?"

"I need some wood to make my puppet. Will you give me some?"

Master Antonio was delighted, and he immediately went to the bench and fetched the piece of wood that had so frightened him. But just as he was about to give it to Geppetto, the piece of wood shook, wriggled violently out of his hands and hit poor Geppetto hard on the shins.

"Is that any way to give a gift, Master Antonio? You almost crippled me!"

"I swear to you that it wasn't me!"

"Are you suggesting that I hit myself?"

"It's the wood!"

"I know that it was the wood, but it was you that hit my legs with it!"

"I did not hit you!"

"Liar!"

"Geppetto, don't insult me, or I'll call you Polendina!"

"Donkey!"

"Polendina!"

"Monkey!"

"Polendina!"

"Baboon!"

"Polendina!"

On hearing himself called Polendina for the third time, Geppetto flew at the carpenter, blind with rage, and they started fighting again.

When they stopped, Master Antonio had two more scratches on his nose, and Geppetto had lost two buttons from his jacket. After the fight ended, they shook hands and again swore to be good friends for the rest of their lives.

Geppetto thanked Master Antonio and limped back home, carrying his piece of wood with him.

{ Chapter 3 }

The puppet is called Pinocchio

Geppetto lived in a small, ground floor room under a staircase. It was simply furnished — a rickety chair, a cheap bed, and an old table. At the end of the room it looked like there was a fireplace with a roaring fire, but it was just a painting. Next to the fire was a painted saucepan that boiled cheerfully, sending out a cloud of steam that looked exactly like real steam.

When he got home, Geppetto took out his tools and began to carve his puppet.

"What name shall I give him?" he said to himself. "I think I'll call him Pinocchio. I'm sure it will bring him luck. I used to know a family called Pinocchio. There was Pinocchio the father, Pinocchia the mother, and Pinocchi the children, and all of them did quite well. The richest of them was a beggar."

Having chosen a name for his puppet, Geppetto started work on him. Soon he had carved the puppet's hair, forehead, and eyes.

He was utterly astonished when he noticed that the eyes he had just finished moved and were looking straight at him.

Geppetto bristled and said in an angry voice, "Wicked wooden eyes, why do you look at me?"

There was no answer.

He began to carve the nose, but as soon as he had finished, it started growing. It

grew, and grew, and grew until it was so huge that it seemed as if it would never end.

Geppetto tried to cut it short, but the more he cut, the longer the nose became.

The mouth was not even finished when it started to laugh and tease Geppetto.

"Stop laughing!" Geppetto scolded, but he might as well have spoken to the wall. "Stop laughing!"

The mouth stopped laughing, but stuck out its tongue as far as it would go.

Geppetto pretended not to notice and carried on working. When the mouth was finished, he carved the chin, throat, shoulders, stomach, arms and hands.

The hands were barely finished when Geppetto's wig was snatched from his head. He turned around and saw his yellow wig in the puppet's hand.

"Pinocchio! Give me back my wig!"

Instead of returning it, Pinocchio put it on his own head, nearly smothering himself.

Pinocchio's insolent behaviour saddened Geppetto more than anything ever had. "You rascal!" he said. "You are not even finished, and you are already showing a lack of respect for your father! That is bad, my boy, very bad!"

And he dried a tear.

The legs and the feet were still to be carved.

When Geppetto finished the feet, he received a kick on the end of his nose.

"I deserve it!" he said to himself. "I should have thought of it sooner! Now it's too late!"

He then took the puppet by the arms and put him on the floor to teach him to walk.

At first, Pinocchio's legs were stiff, and he could not move, but Geppetto held his hand and showed him how to put one foot in front of the other.

Once his legs were more flexible, Pinocchio began to walk by himself and to run around the room. As soon as he noticed that the front door was open, he ran through it and escaped down the street.

Geppetto rushed after him but could not catch up. Pinocchio ran as fast as a hare, knocking his wooden feet against the pavement and making as much noise as twenty pairs of clogs.

"Stop him! Stop him!" shouted Geppetto. But the people in the street, seeing a wooden puppet running like a racehorse, stood still, utterly amazed, and laughed, and laughed, and laughed.

At last, a policeman arrived. He thought a horse must have escaped from its master, so he stood bravely in the middle of the road with his legs apart, determined to stop it and prevent any worse disasters.

When Pinocchio saw the policeman barricading the street, he tried to take him by surprise and run between his legs. The policeman managed to grab him by the nose — it was a ridiculously huge nose that seemed as if it had been specially designed for policemen to grab — and returned him to Geppetto. Geppetto intended to pull Pinocchio's ears to punish him. But his ears were nowhere to be found! And do you know why? In his hurry to carve the puppet, Geppetto had forgotten to make them.

So Geppetto took him by the collar, and as he was leading him away, he said, "Just wait 'til we get home! I'll teach you such a lesson."

When Pinocchio heard this, he threw himself on the ground and refused to go any further. A crowd of curious spectators immediately gathered around them.

"Poor puppet!" said some of the spectators. "He's right not to want to go home! Who knows how that bad old man will beat him!"

And others added, "Geppetto seems a good man. But he can be very strict with boys. If that poor puppet is left with him, he is quite capable of tearing him apart!"

They all said so much that the policeman let Pinocchio go and dragged Geppetto off to prison. The poor man, unable to defend himself, cried like a calf, and as he was being led away, he wailed, "Wretched boy! And to think that I worked so hard to make him a well-behaved puppet! It serves me right! I should have thought of it sooner!"

What happened afterwards is a story that is quite beyond belief, but I shall tell it to you in the following chapters.

{ *Chapter 4* }

Pinocchio meets the talking grasshopper

hile Geppetto was being taken to prison, through no fault of his own, Pinocchio, finally free from the policeman, ran away as fast as he could. In his hurry to get home, he rushed across the fields as quickly as a hunted rabbit, jumping high banks, thorn hedges, and ditches full of water.

When he got home, the front door was ajar. He pushed it open, went in, and, after locking the door behind him, he sat down on the floor with a great sigh of relief.

But his satisfaction did not last long. He heard someone in the room saying, "Cri-cri-cri!"

"Who's that?" said a frightened Pinocchio.

"It is me!"

Pinocchio turned around and saw a big grasshopper crawling slowly up the wall.

"Who are you?"

"I am the talking grasshopper, and I have lived in this room for over a hundred years."

"Well, now this room is mine," said Pinocchio. "So do me a favour and go away right now and don't come back."

"I won't go," answered the grasshopper, "until I have told you a great truth."

"Go on then, but be quick about it."

"Children who rebel against their parents and run away from home will always get into trouble. They will never come to any good in this world, and sooner or later, they will bitterly repent."

"Say what you like, Grasshopper, but I have already made up my mind. I am going to run away tomorrow, at dawn, because if I stay here I'll suffer the same fate as all other boys. I'll be sent to school. And to tell you the truth, I do not want to learn. It's much more fun to run after butterflies, or to climb trees and take baby birds from their nests."

"Poor little fool! Don't you realize that if all you do is play, you'll grow up to be a complete donkey, and that everyone will make fun of you?"

"Shut up, you wicked grasshopper!" shouted Pinocchio.

But instead of becoming angry at Pinocchio's bad behaviour, the patient, wise grasshopper, continued in the same tone. "If you don't want to go to school, then why not learn a trade, at least then you would be able to earn an honest living!"

"I'll tell you why," replied Pinocchio, who was beginning to lose his patience. "Of all the trades in the world, there is only one that I really like the sound of."

"And what is that?"

"To eat, drink, sleep and have fun, and to lead a drifter's life all day long."

"Generally," said the talking grasshopper with the same composure, "anyone who follows that trade almost always ends up either in the hospital or in prison."

"Be careful, you wicked croaker! You are in trouble if I become angry!"

"Poor Pinocchio. I really pity you!"

"Why?"

"Because you are a puppet, and — even worse — you have a wooden head."

At these words Pinocchio jumped up in a rage, grabbed a mallet from the bench, and threw it at the talking cricket.

He may not have meant to hit him, but unfortunately the mallet struck the grasshopper right on the head. The poor creature scarcely had time to cry, "Cri-cri-cri," and there he was, flattened against the wall.

{ Chapter 5 }

Pinocchio makes a strange omelette

ight soon fell, and remembering that he had not eaten all day, Pinocchio began to feel a gnawing in his stomach that was very much like an appetite.

But boys' appetites grow fast, and soon his appetite became a terrible hunger, and this hunger quickly became a ravenous beast.

Poor Pinocchio ran to the fireplace to eat the contents of the boiling saucepan he saw there, but it was just a painting. Pinocchio was very surprised. His nose, which was already rather long, grew at least three inches longer.

Then he began to run around the room, looking everywhere in the hope of finding a bit of dry bread, a crust, a dog's bone, a little mouldy pudding, a fish bone, a cherry pip – just anything that he could eat. But he found absolutely nothing.

Poor Pinocchio got hungrier and hungrier. His only relief was yawning, and his yawns were so huge that sometimes his mouth almost reached to where his ears ought to have been. After he yawned, he was even more ravenous and felt as if he might faint.

Then he began to cry desperately and said, "The talking grasshopper was right. I was wrong to rebel against my father and to run away from home. If my father were here now, I would not be dying of hunger! Oh hunger, is the most dreadful thing!"

Just then, he thought he saw something in a pile of wood shavings — it was round and white and looked like a hen's egg. He leaped to his feet and grabbed it. It was an egg!

Pinocchio was so happy but, worried that it was all a dream, he kept turning the egg over and over in his hands, feeling it and kissing it. "But how will I cook it?" he wondered. "Should I make an omelette? Would it be tastier to poach? Or should I just boil it? No, the quickest way is to fry it and I am in such a hurry to eat!"

He quickly built a small fire and put the pan over it. Instead of oil or butter, he poured some water into the pan, and when it started to steam, he broke the egg over it so that the contents would land in the pan. But instead of egg white and yolk, a very friendly little chicken popped out. The chicken bowed and said, "A thousand thanks for saving me the trouble of breaking the shell, Master Pinocchio. Look after youself, and give my best to your family!"

Then the chicken spread its wings, darted through the window, and flew away.

The poor puppet stood there as if bewitched, with his eyes fixed, his mouth open, and the empty shell still in his hand. As he regained his senses, he began to howl and stamp his feet in desperation.

"Oh! The talking grasshopper was right. If I had not run away from home, and if my father were here now, I would not be dying of hunger! Oh, hunger is a dreadful thing!"

His stomach growled more than ever, and he did not know how to stop it. He decided he would leave the house and walk around the town in the hope of finding a kind person who might give him some food.

Chapter 6

Pinocchio's feet are burned off

t was a wild and stormy night. Thunder crashed, and the lightning was so violent that the sky seemed to be on fire. A blustery wind whistled angrily and swept clouds of dust across the countryside, making the trees creak and groan.

Pinocchio was terrified of thunder, but his hunger was greater than his fear. He closed the front door behind him and ran to the town, which he soon reached, panting, with his tongue hanging out like a dog's.

But the town was dark and deserted. The shops were closed, the windows shut, and there was not so much as a dog in the street. It seemed like the land of the dead.

Driven by desperation and hunger, Pinocchio rang the bell of the first house he came to, saying to himself, "Somebody will answer."

A little old man appeared at a window with a nightcap on his head, and called to him angrily, "What do you want at this hour?"

"Would you be kind enough to give me some bread?"

"Wait there. I'll come right back," said the little old man, thinking he was dealing with one of those rascally boys who have fun at night ringing the doorbells of respectable people to get them out of bed.

After half a minute, the same little old man shouted to Pinocchio, "Stand

underneath the window and hold out your cap."

Pinocchio took off his cap; but just as he held it out, an enormous bowl of water was poured over him, drenching him from head to foot.

He returned home like a wet chicken, quite exhausted. No longer having the strength to stand, he sat down and rested his damp and muddy feet on the warm stove.

Then he fell asleep. And while he slept, his feet, which were wooden, caught fire and they burned away slowly.

Pinocchio continued to sleep and snore as if his feet belonged to someone else. At last, around dawn, he was woken up by a knocking at the door.

"Who's there?" he asked, yawning and rubbing his eyes.

"It's me!" answered a voice.

It was the voice of Geppetto.

{ Chapter 7 }

Geppetto gives the puppet something to eat

oor Pinocchio, still half asleep, had not yet discovered that his feet
had been burned off. When he heard his father's voice, he slipped
off his stool to run and open the door. But instead, he stumbled and fell flat on the
floor, making as much noise as if a sack of wooden spoons had been thrown from a
fifth floor window.

"Open the door!" shouted Geppetto from the street.

"Dear Father, I can't," answered the puppet, crying and rolling around on the floor.

"Why not?"

"Because my feet have been eaten."

"And who has eaten your feet?"

"The cat," said Pinocchio, seeing the cat, who was amusing herself playing with some
wood shavings.

"Open the door, I tell you!" demanded Geppetto. "If you don't, when I get into
the house I will beat you!"

"I can't stand up, believe me. Oh, poor me! Poor me! I'll have to walk on my knees
for the rest of my life!"

Thinking that Pinocchio's cries were just another one of his tricks, Geppetto

climbed up the wall and got in through a window.

He was very angry, and at first he did nothing but tell the puppet off. But when he saw Pinocchio lying on the ground without feet, he was overcome with pity. He picked him up, kissed him, and reassured him. And as the tears ran down his cheeks, he cried, "My dear little Pinocchio! How did you manage to burn your feet?"

"I don't know, Father, but believe me, it has been a horrible night — one that I'll never forget. It thundered and lightninged, and I was very hungry. And then the talking grasshopper said to me, 'It serves you right! You have been wicked and you deserve it.' And I said to him, 'Be careful, grasshopper!' And he said, 'You are a puppet, and you have a wooden head,' and then I threw a mallet at him and he died, but it was his own fault. I didn't want to kill him, but I did, and then a chicken flew out and said, 'Give my best to your family!' Then I got even hungrier, and a little old man in a nightcap said to me, 'Stand underneath the window and hold out your cap', then he poured a bowl of water on my head. I came home, and because I was still very hungry, I put my feet on the stove to dry them, and then you returned. Now my feet are burned off, and I am still hungry, but I don't have any feet any more!" Poor Pinocchio began to cry so loudly that he could be heard a mile away.

From this jumbled account, Geppetto had only understood that the puppet was dying of hunger. He took three pears from his pocket, gave them to Pinocchio, and said, "I was going to eat these pears for breakfast, but I will give them to you instead. I hope they will make you feel better."

"If you want me to eat them, please peel them for me."

"Peel them?" said Geppetto, astonished. "I should never have thought that you were so fussy. That is bad! In this world you must learn to eat everything as you never know what you may be given."

"You may be right," interrupted Pinocchio, "but I won't eat fruit that has not been peeled. I can't stand the skin."

So, Geppetto fetched a knife and patiently peeled the three pears and put the peelings on a corner of the table.

After eating the first pear in two mouthfuls, Pinocchio was about to throw away the core, but Geppetto grabbed his arm. "Don't throw that away," he said. "In this world, everything may be of use."

"But I certainly won't eat the core!" shouted the puppet, turning on him like a viper.

"Very well," Geppetto replied, without losing his temper.

And so the three cores, instead of being thrown out of the window, were put on a corner of the table along with the peelings.

Having eaten, or rather having devoured, the three pears, Pinocchio yawned and said fretfully, "I am as hungry as ever!"

"But I have nothing else to give you!"

"Nothing?"

"I only have the peelings and the cores of the three pears."

"Well, then!" said Pinocchio. "If there is nothing else, I'll eat some peelings."

And he began to eat them. At first he made a sour face, but then he quickly swallowed the pear skins one after the other. Then he ate the cores. And when he had eaten everything in sight, he put his hands on his hips and said joyfully, "Ah! Now I feel better."

"You see?" said Geppetto. "I was right when I said that everything may be of use in this world. We can never know, my dear boy, what may happen to us!"

{ Chapter 8 }

Geppetto sells his coat to buy a spelling book

s soon as Pinocchio had satisfied his hunger, he began to cry and grumble because he wanted a pair of new feet.

To punish Pinocchio for being naughty, Geppetto left him to cry for half the day. He then said to him, "Why should I make you new feet? So that you can run away from home again?"

"I promise," sobbed the puppet, "that from now on, I will be good."

"All children," replied Geppetto, "say the same thing when they want something."

"I promise to go to school and to study so that you will be proud of me."

"When they want something, all children repeat the same story."

"But I'm not like other children! I'm better than all of them, and I always speak the truth. I promise you, Father, that I will learn a trade, and that I'll look after you in your old age."

Although he put on a serious face, Geppetto's eyes were full of tears, and his heart was so sad at seeing poor Pinocchio in such a state. He did not say another word but, taking his tools and two small pieces of well-seasoned wood, he set to work.

In less than an hour, the feet were finished — two little feet so beautiful they might have been carved by a great sculptor.

Geppetto then said to the puppet, "Shut your eyes and go to sleep!"

Pinocchio shut his eyes and pretended to be asleep.

And while the puppet pretended to sleep, Geppetto, with some glue that he had melted in an eggshell, stuck the feet in place. He did such a good job that nothing could be seen of where the feet were joined.

As soon as the puppet realized that he had feet again, he jumped down from the table where he was lying and began to leap around the room, mad with delight.

"To thank you for what you have done for me," said Pinocchio to his father, "I will go to school at once."

"Good boy."

"But to go to school, I'll need some clothes."

Geppetto, who was poor and did not even have a penny in his pocket, made the puppet a little suit with flowered paper, a pair of shoes with tree bark and a bread dough cap.

Pinocchio ran to look at his reflection in a pot of water and was so pleased with it that he strutted around like a peacock and said, "I look like a gentleman!"

"You do," answered Geppetto. "It is not fine clothes but clean clothes that make the gentleman."

"By the way," added the puppet, "I can't go to school without a spelling book."

"You're right. But what will we do to get one?"

"That's easy. We'll go to the bookseller and buy it."

"And the money?"

"I have none."

"Neither do I," added the old man sadly.

Pinocchio, although he was a very happy boy, became sad too, because even children understand real poverty.

"Just a moment!" said Geppetto, suddenly getting up, putting on his old, patched coat and running out of the house.

He returned shortly with a spelling book for Pinocchio, but the old coat was gone. Poor Geppetto was wearing only his shirt, even though it was snowing outside.

"Where's your coat, Father?"

"I sold it."

"Why?"

"Because it made me too warm."

Pinocchio understood at once and leaped up and threw his arms round Geppetto's neck, and kissed him again and again.

{ Chapter 9 }

Pinocchio sells his spelling book to see a show

s soon as it stopped snowing, Pinocchio left for school with his spelling book under his arm. On the way, he began to imagine lots of things in his little head, and to make wonderful plans, each one even better than the one before.

"Today at school I'll learn to read," he said to himself. "Then tomorrow I'll learn to write, and the day after tomorrow to do sums. Then with my skills I'll make lots of money, and with the first pennies I earn, I'll buy a beautiful cloth coat for my father. But what am I saying? Cloth! It will be made of gold and silver with diamond buttons. That poor man really deserves it. He is wearing only his shirt so that he could buy me books and send me to school. And it is so cold! Only a father would make such a sacrifice."

At that moment, Pinocchio thought he heard music in the distance. It sounded like fifes and the beating of a big drum: *fi-fi-fi, fi-fi-fi, zum, zum, zum, zum.*

He stopped and listened. The sounds came from the end of a street that led to an open square on the seashore.

"What is that music? What a shame that I have to go to school . . ."

Pinocchio hesitated, trying to decide what to do — whether to go to school, or to go and listen to the music.

"Today I'll go and hear the music," he decided at last, "and tomorrow I'll go to school."

As he ran, the sound of the fifes and the beating of the big drum became clearer: *fi-fi-fi, zum, zum, zum, zum.*

Soon he found himself in the middle of a square full of people, who were all crowding around a multi-coloured building that was made of wood and canvas.

"What is that building?" Pinocchio asked a little boy standing nearby.

"Read the sign, and then you'll know."

"I would read it, but it so happens that today I don't know how to read."

"Well done, blockhead! Then I'll read it for you. The writing on the sign says, '*Great Puppet Theatre.*'"

"When does the play begin?"

"Right now."

"How much does it cost to get in?"

"Five pennies."

In his curiosity, Pinocchio lost all control and said to the boy, "Would you lend me five pennies 'til tomorrow?"

"Usually I would lend it to you happily," said the boy, "but today I cannot."

"I'll sell you my jacket for five pennies," said Pinocchio.

"Why would I want a jacket made with flowered paper? If it rained, and the paper got wet, it would be impossible to get it off my back."

"Will you buy my shoes?"

"They would only be good to light a fire with."

"How much will you give me for my cap?"

"That would be a fine bargain! A cap made with bread dough! Mice would

probably eat it right off my head."

Pinocchio was on tenterhooks. He was about to make another offer, but he did not have the courage. He hesitated. And finally said, "Will you give me five pennies for this new spelling book?"

"I never buy anything like that from other children," replied the boy, who had much more sense than Pinocchio.

"I'll buy the spelling book for five pennies," called a street trader, who had been listening to their conversation.

The book was sold there and then. And to think that poor Geppetto, shivering at home, had sold his coat to buy his son a spelling book!

{ Chapter 10 }

The show puppets welcome Pinocchio

When Pinocchio walked into the little puppet theatre, something happened that nearly caused a riot.

The curtain was up, and the play had already begun.

On the stage, two puppets, Harlequin and Punchinello, were arguing with each other – standard practice in puppet plays – and threatening to come to blows at any moment.

The audience cried with laughter as they listened to the two puppets bickering. They gestured and abused each other so naturally that they could have been two real people.

Then, suddenly, Harlequin stopped and turned to the audience. He pointed to someone right down in the pit of the theatre and exclaimed dramatically, "My goodness! Am I dreaming, or am I awake? Surely that is Pinocchio!"

"It is Pinocchio!" cried Punchinello.

"It certainly is!" cried Miss Rose, peeping from behind the curtains.

"It's Pinocchio! It's Pinocchio!" shouted all the puppets together, leaping from all directions onto the stage. "It's our brother Pinocchio! Long live Pinocchio!"

"Pinocchio, come up here," cried Harlequin, "come into the arms of your puppet brothers!"

At this friendly invitation, Pinocchio leaped from the end of the pit into the reserved seats. Another leap landed him on the orchestra leader's head, and a final jump put him on the stage.

The kisses, the hugs, the friendly pinches, and the warm, brotherly affection that Pinocchio received from the actors and actresses in the puppet company were beyond comparison.

It was very moving, but the audience, realizing the play had stopped, became impatient and began to shout, "We want the play! Go on with the play!"

But instead of continuing the performance, the puppets made even more noise, put Pinocchio on their shoulders and carried him triumphantly in front of the footlights.

At that moment, the Showman appeared. He was very big and so ugly that the sight of him was enough to frighten anyone. His beard was as black as ink and so long that it reached from his chin to the ground and he often trod on it when he walked. His mouth was as big as an oven and his eyes were like two red glass lanterns with lights burning inside them. He carried a large whip made with snakes and foxes' tails twisted together, which he cracked constantly.

At his unexpected appearance, there was silence. No one dared to breathe. A fly could have been heard in the stillness and the poor puppets trembled like leaves.

"Why have you come to cause trouble in my theatre?" the Showman asked Pinocchio in a gruff voice that made him sound like a goblin with a bad cold.

"Believe me, honoured sir, it was not my fault!"

"Enough! We will settle the score tonight."

As soon as the play was over, the Showman went into the kitchen, where a fine sheep was being spit-roasted for his supper. There was not enough wood to finish roasting and browning it, so he called Harlequin and Punchinello and said to them, "Bring that puppet here. You will find him hanging on a nail. He looks like he is made of very dry wood and I'm sure that if he was thrown on the fire, he would make a beautiful blaze for my roast."

At first, Harlequin and Punchinello hesitated, but a glance from their master made them obey. They returned to the kitchen carrying poor Pinocchio, who was wriggling like an eel and crying in despair, "Father! Father! Save me! I don't want to die! I don't want to die!"

{ Chapter 11 }

The Showman sneezes and pardons Pinocchio

Fire-Eater, the Showman, looked like a terrible man, especially because of his enormous black beard. But in fact, he had a good heart. When poor Pinocchio was brought in, struggling and screaming, "I don't want to die! I don't want to die!" Fire-Eater felt sorry for him. He tried to put his feelings for the puppet aside as long as he could, but soon he could not stand it any longer, and he sneezed violently. When Harlequin, who until then was in total despair, heard the sneeze, he became quite cheerful. Leaning towards Pinocchio, he whispered, "Good news, brother! The Showman has sneezed, and that is a sign that he pities you, so you are saved!"

While most men weep, or at least pretend to dry their eyes when they feel compassion for somebody, Fire-Eater sneezed whenever he was overcome with emotion.

After he sneezed, the Showman shouted to Pinocchio, "Stop crying! Your wailing has given me a pain in my stomach. I feel a spasm that almost — *Achoo! Achoo!*"

"Bless you!" said Pinocchio.

"Thank you. And your father and mother, are they still alive?" asked Fire-Eater.

"My father is. But I never knew my mother."

"It would be so sad for your poor old father if I were to have you thrown into those burning coals! Poor old man! I feel so sorry for him! *Achoo! Achoo! Achoo!*"

"Bless you!" said Pinocchio.

"Thank you. All the same, I deserve some sympathy. As you see, I have no more wood to finish roasting my sheep, and to tell you the truth, under the circumstances, you would have been perfect! However, I have had pity on you, so I must not complain. Instead, I will burn one of the puppets in my company. Guards!"

Two wooden guards immediately responded to his call. They were very tall and very thin. They wore hats on their heads, and held unsheathed swords in their hands.

"Take Harlequin, bind him tightly, and throw him on the fire," the Showman ordered. "My sheep must be well roasted."

Poor Harlequin! He was so terrified that his legs gave way, and he fell face first onto the ground.

When he saw this, Pinocchio threw himself at the Showman's feet and, shedding tears all over his long beard, he pleaded, "Have pity, Sir Fire-Eater!"

"There are no sirs here," the Showman answered severely.

"Have pity, Sir Knight!"

"There are no knights here!"

"Have pity, Commander!"

"There are no commanders here!"

"Have pity, your Excellence!"

On hearing himself called "Excellence," the Showman began to smile, immediately becoming kinder and more agreeable. He turned to Pinocchio and asked, "Well, what do you want from me?"

"I beg you to pardon poor Harlequin."

"For him there can be no pardon. As I have spared you, so he must be put on the fire. My sheep must be well roasted."

"In that case," cried Pinocchio proudly, as he stood up and threw his cap to the floor, "in that case, I know what I must do. Come, guards! Tie me up and throw me into the fire. It's not right that poor Harlequin, my true friend, should die for me!"

Pinocchio's brave words made all the puppets who were there cry. Even the guards wept like babies.

At first, Fire-Eater remained as cold and hard as ice, but little by little he began to melt — and to sneeze. After sneezing four or five times, he opened his arms affectionately and said to Pinocchio, "You are a good, brave boy! Come here and give me a kiss."

Pinocchio ran to him, climbed up the Showman's beard and deposited a big kiss on the end of his nose.

"Then the pardon is granted?" asked poor Harlequin in a very faint voice.

"The pardon is granted!" answered Fire-Eater. "Very well, then!" he added sighing and shaking his head. "Tonight I'll have to eat my sheep half-cooked. But next time, anyone who stands in my way is in trouble!"

When they found out about the pardon, all the puppets ran to the stage, lit the lamps and the chandeliers as if for a full performance, and began to dance. At dawn, they were still dancing.

{ Chapter 12 }

Fire-Eater becomes generous

he next day, Fire-Eater called Pinocchio aside and asked him, "What is your father's name?"

"Geppetto."

"And what is his trade?"

"That of a very poor man."

"Does he earn much?"

"Earn much? He never has a penny in his pocket. To buy a spelling book for me, he sold his only coat — a coat so patched it was not fit to be seen."

"Poor fellow! I feel almost sorry for him! Here are five gold pieces. Go at once and take them to him with my compliments."

Pinocchio thanked the Showman, embraced all of the puppets one by one, even the guards, and then set out for home, feeling very happy.

But he had not gone far when he met a lame fox and a cat who was blind in both eyes. They were helping each other along like good friends. The fox leaned on the cat, and the cat was guided by the fox.

"Good day, Pinocchio," said the fox, bowing politely.

"How do you know my name?" asked the puppet.

"I know your father well."

"Where did you see him?"

"I saw him yesterday at the door of his house."

"And what was he doing?"

"He was only wearing his shirt and was shivering with cold."

"Poor Father! But after today, he will shiver no more!"

"Why?"

"Because I have become a gentleman."

"A gentleman? You?" said the fox, and he began to laugh rudely and scornfully. The cat began to laugh too, but she combed her whiskers with her front paws to hide it.

"There's nothing to laugh at," cried Pinocchio angrily. "I don't want to make you jealous, but as you can see, I have five gold pieces."

And he pulled out the money that Fire-Eater had given him.

At the pleasing ring of the money, the fox involuntarily stretched out the paw that had just moments ago seemed crippled, and the cat opened wide two eyes that looked like green lanterns. But she shut them again so quickly that Pinocchio did not notice.

"And now," asked the fox, "what are you going to do with all that money?"

"First," answered the puppet, "I intend to buy a new coat for my father, made from gold and silver, with diamond buttons, and then I'll buy a spelling book for myself."

"For yourself?"

"Yes indeed, for I intend to go to school and study like a good boy."

"Look at me!" said the fox. "Through my foolish passion for study I have lost a leg."

"Look at me!" said the cat. "Through my foolish passion for study I have lost the sight in both my eyes."

At that moment, a blackbird, perched on a hedge by the road, began to sing, and said, "Pinocchio, don't listen to the advice of bad companions. If you do, you'll be sorry!"

Poor blackbird! If only he had not spoken! With a great leap, the cat sprang at him, and without even giving him time to say "Oh", ate him in a mouthful, feathers and all.

After eating him and cleaning her mouth, the cat shut her eyes again and seemed

as blind as ever.

"Poor blackbird!" said Pinocchio to the cat. "Why did you do that?"

"I did it to teach him a lesson. Next time he won't interfere in other people's conversations."

They had gone almost halfway to Pinocchio's house when the fox stopped suddenly and said to the puppet, "Would you like to double your money?"

"In what way?"

"Would you like to turn your five miserable gold pieces into a hundred, a thousand, two thousand?"

"Yes, definitely! But how?"

"It's easy enough. Instead of returning home, you must come with us."

"And where do you want to take me?"

"To the Land of Fools."

Pinocchio thought for a moment, and then said firmly, "No, I won't go. I'm nearly home, so I'll go back to my father, who is waiting for me. Who knows how the poor old man must have suffered yesterday when I didn't come back! I have been a bad son. The talking grasshopper was right when he said, 'Disobedient children never come to any good in this world.' To learn that lesson has cost me a great deal, for many bad things have happened to me. Even yesterday, in Fire-Eater's house, I was almost . . . Oh! It makes me shudder just to think of it!"

"Well, then," said the fox, "you're quite sure you want to go home? Go, then, and so much the worse for you."

"So much the worse for you!" repeated the cat.

"Think about it carefully, Pinocchio, for you are throwing away a fortune."

"A fortune!" repeated the cat.

"Between today and tomorrow your five gold pieces would have become two thousand."

"Two thousand!" repeated the cat.

"But how is that possible?" asked Pinocchio, his mouth wide open in astonishment.

"I'll explain it to you at once," said the fox. "You must know that in the Land of

Fools there is a sacred field called the Field of Miracles. In this field, you dig a little hole, and you put into it, we'll say, one gold piece. You cover up the hole with a little dirt, water it with two pails of water from the fountain, sprinkle it with two pinches of salt, and then, when night comes, you go quietly to bed. During the night, the gold piece will grow and flower and in the morning, when you get up and go back to the field, you'll find a beautiful tree laden with as many gold pieces as an ear of corn has kernels in July."

"Suppose," said Pinocchio, more and more bewildered, "that I buried my five gold pieces in that field. How many would I find the following morning?"

"That is an easy calculation," replied the fox, "a calculation that you can make on the ends of your fingers. If every gold piece gives you an increase of five hundred. Multiply five hundred by five, and the following morning you would find two thousand five hundred shining gold pieces in your pocket."

"Oh! How wonderful!" cried Pinocchio, dancing for joy. "As soon as I've collected those gold pieces, I'll keep two thousand for myself and give the other five hundred to both of you."

"A present to us?" cried the fox, sounding very offended. "Don't be absurd!"

"Don't be absurd!" repeated the cat.

"We don't work for our own gain," said the fox. "We work only to enrich the lives of others."

"Others!" repeated the cat.

"What good people!" thought Pinocchio. And instantly forgetting his father, the new coat, the spelling book, and all his good resolutions, he said to the fox and the cat, "Let's leave at once! I'll go with you."

{ Chapter 13 }

Pinocchio and his companions stop at the Lobster Inn

They walked and walked and walked until at last, towards evening, they arrived at the Lobster Inn.

"Let's stop here for a while," said the fox, "we can have something to eat and rest for an hour or two. We'll start again at midnight, so we can arrive at the Field of Miracles early tomorrow morning."

They walked into the inn and sat down at a table, but none of them were hungry.

The cat, who had indigestion and was not feeling well at all, managed to eat only thirty-five small fish with tomato sauce and four portions of tripe with Parmesan cheese. And she asked three times for the grated butter and cheese because she thought the tripe did not have enough flavour!

The fox, too, would happily have nibbled just a little snack, but his doctor had put him on a strict diet. He was forced to be content with a hare dressed with sweet and sour sauce, garnished lightly with fat chickens and young hens. After the hare, he sent for a casserole of partridges, rabbits, frogs, lizards, and other delicacies, but he would not touch anything else. He was so disgusted by the sight of food, he said, that he could eat nothing more.

Pinocchio ate the least. He asked for some walnuts and bread, but he left everything on his plate. The poor boy, whose thoughts were fixed on the Field of Miracles, had come down with a case of mental indigestion just thinking about the gold pieces.

After supper, the fox said to the innkeeper, "Give us two good rooms, one for Mr Pinocchio, and the other for me and my companion. We will catch a little sleep before we leave. But remember that we need to be called at midnight so we can continue with our journey."

"Yes, gentlemen," answered the innkeeper and winked at the fox and the cat as if to say, "I know what you're up to. We understand one another!"

As soon as Pinocchio got into bed, he fell asleep and began to dream. He dreamed that he was in the middle of a field, and the field was full of bushes covered with gold pieces that clinked in the wind as if to say, "Whoever wants us, come and take us." But when Pinocchio was at the best bit – just as he was stretching out his hand to pick handfuls of those beautiful gold pieces and put them in his pocket – he was woken up suddenly by three violent knocks on the door of his room.

It was the innkeeper, who had come to tell him that it was already midnight.

"Are my friends ready?" asked the puppet.

"Ready? Why, they left two hours ago."

"Why were they in such a hurry?"

"Because the cat received a message that her eldest kitten was ill with swollen feet and was in danger of dying."

"Did they pay for supper?"

"What a question! They are too well-educated to dream of offering such an insult to a gentleman like you."

"What a pity! It's an insult that I would have welcomed!" said Pinocchio, scratching his head. He then asked, "And where did my good friends say they would wait for me?"

"At the Field of Miracles, tomorrow morning, at dawn."

Pinocchio paid one gold piece for his supper, and that of the fox and the cat, and left.

It was so dark outside the inn that the puppet could not even see his hand in front of his face and had to grope his way along. In the surrounding countryside, everything was still. Pinocchio was startled by some night birds as they flew past him and brushed his nose with their wings. He leaped back in fright and shouted, "Who goes there?" The hills echoed with his voice, "Who goes there? Who goes there? Who goes there?"

As he walked on, he saw a little insect shining dimly on the trunk of a tree. It looked like a nightlight with a shade made of transparent china.

"Who are you?" asked Pinocchio.

"I am the ghost of the talking grasshopper," answered the insect in a low voice so weak and faint that it seemed to come from another world.

"What do you want with me?"

"I want to give you some advice. Go home and take the four gold pieces that you have left to your poor father. He is weeping with despair because you have not returned."

"Tomorrow my father will be a rich gentleman, for these four gold pieces will have become two thousand."

"My boy, don't put your trust in those who promise to make you rich in a day — they are either fools or scoundrels! Listen to me, and go home."

"No, I'm determined to go on."

"The hour is late!"

"I'm determined to go on."

"The night is dark!"

"I'm determined to go on."

"The road is dangerous!"

"I'm determined to go on."

"Remember that children who are determined to do as they please and have their own way regret it sooner or later."

"Always the same stories. Good night ."

"Good night, Pinocchio, and may Heaven save you from dangers and assassins."

The talking grasshopper vanished suddenly, like a light that has been blown out, and the road became darker than ever.

{ Chapter 14 }

The puppet falls among assassins

"Really," said the puppet to himself as he started his journey again, "us poor children are very unfortunate. Everybody tells us off, everybody admonishes us, everybody gives us advice. The way they talk, they think they are our fathers and our masters — all of them, even the talking grasshopper! Because I chose not to listen to that tiresome grasshopper, who knows how many bad things will happen to me. I'll even meet assassins! That does not matter, though, because I don't believe in assassins — I've never believed in them. I think that assassins were invented by fathers to frighten boys who want to go out at night. Besides, suppose I were to come across them in the road. Do you think they would frighten me? Not at all. I would walk up to them and say, 'Gentlemen assassins, what do you want with me? Remember that with me there is no joking. Go about your business and be quiet!' If those poor assassins heard me speaking in such a determined way, they would run away at once. If they didn't run away, then I would run away myself, and that would be the end of it."

But Pinocchio did not have time to finish his reasoning, because he was interrupted by a slight rustling of leaves behind him.

He turned to look, and saw two evil-looking black figures completely covered in coal sacks. They were running after him on tiptoe, taking huge leaps like two phantoms.

"They are really here!" he said to himself, and not knowing where to hide his gold pieces, he put them under his tongue.

Then he tried to escape. But before he could take a step, he was grabbed by the arm and heard two terrifying voices saying to him, "Your money or your life!"

Unable to answer in words properly because of the money in his mouth, Pinocchio bowed and gestured to try to make the two cloaked figures, whose eyes were visible only through holes in their sacks, understand that he was a poor puppet, and that he did not even have a forged coin in his pocket.

"Come now! Less nonsense and out with the money!" cried the two bandits threateningly.

And the puppet made a gesture with his hands as if to say, "I don't have any."

"Hand over your money or you are dead," said the taller of the two.

"Dead!" repeated the other.

"And after we kill you, we'll kill your father, too."

"Your father!"

"No, no, not my poor father!" cried Pinocchio. And as he said it, the gold pieces clinked in his mouth.

"Ah! You rascal! You've hidden the money under your tongue! Spit it out at once!"

But Pinocchio did not.

"Ah! You pretend to be deaf, do you? Wait a minute and we'll find a way to make you spit it out."

One of them grabbed the puppet by the end of his nose, and the other took him by the chin, and they pulled in opposite directions, one up and the other down, to force Pinocchio to open his mouth, but it was no use. His mouth seemed to be nailed shut.

Then the shorter assassin took out a knife and tried to force it between Pinocchio's lips. But Pinocchio, quick as a flash, caught the assassin's hand in his teeth, bit it clean off, and spat it out. He was utterly astonished when he saw that he had spat out a cat's paw, not a hand!

Encouraged by this, Pinocchio gave such a sudden twist that it freed him from his attackers. He jumped over the hedge by the road, and started to run across the fields. The assassins ran after him like two dogs chasing a hare. The one who had lost a paw ran on one leg, though how he did it is a mystery.

After running for miles, Pinocchio was exhausted and lost. He climbed a very tall pine tree and sat high up in the branches. The assassins tried to climb after him, but halfway up the trunk, they slid down, landing on the ground with skinned hands and feet.

But they did not give up so easily. They gathered some dry wood, piled it underneath the tree, and set fire to it. In no time at all the tree was on fire. The flames rose higher and higher and Pinocchio, not wanting to end his life like a roasted pigeon, made a spectacular leap from the top of the tree and started running across the fields and vineyards. The assassins followed close behind him without slowing.

At dawn, they were still chasing him. Suddenly Pinocchio's way was blocked by a wide, deep ditch full of dirty coffee-coloured water. "One! Two! Three!" cried the puppet, and making a run up to the ditch, he jumped to the other side. The assassins also jumped, but misjudged the distance – splash! splash! – and fell right in the middle of the ditch. Pinocchio heard the splashing water and laughingly shouted, "A fine bath to you, gentlemen assassins!"

Pinocchio was sure they had drowned but when he turned to look, they were both running after him, still in their sacks, water dripping from them as if they had each sprung a leak.

{ Chapter 15 }

Pinocchio is hanged

Pinocchio was close to throwing himself on the ground and giving up. However, as he looked around he saw a small white house standing out among the dark green trees.

"If only I could get to that house," he said to himself, "I might be saved."

Without delaying, he ran for his life with the assassins still close behind.

After running for nearly two hours, he finally arrived at the house.

He knocked, but no one answered.

He knocked again, much louder, as he could hear the sound of footsteps approaching, and the heavy panting of his pursuers. Still no one answered.

In desperation he started to kick and pound the door with all his strength. Suddenly the window opened and a beautiful child appeared. She had blue hair and a face as white as a waxen image; her eyes were closed and her hands were crossed on her breast. Without moving her lips, she said in a voice that seemed to come from another world, "In this house there is no one. They are all dead."

"Then at least open the door for me yourself," Pinocchio pleaded.

"I'm dead, too."

"Dead? Then what are you doing at the window?"

"I'm waiting for my coffin to come and carry me away."

Having said this, she disappeared, and the window closed noiselessly.

"Oh! Beautiful child with blue hair," said Pinocchio, "open the door for pity's sake! Have compassion on a poor boy who is being chased by assas . . ."

But before he could finish, he was grabbed by the collar, and the same two horrible voices said to him threateningly, "You won't escape from us again!"

Fearing that his end was near, the puppet trembled so violently that the joints of his wooden legs began to creak, and the gold pieces hidden under his tongue clinked.

"Now then," demanded the assassins, "will you open your mouth? Yes or no? Ah! No answer? Leave it to us. This time we'll force you to open it!"

They drew out two long, horrid knives as sharp as razors — slash! slash! — and tried to stab him twice.

But luckily for him, Pinocchio was made of very hard wood. The knife blades shattered, and the assassins were left with only the handles in their hands, staring at each other.

"I know what we need to do," said one of them. "He must be hanged! Let's hang him!"

"Hang him!" repeated the other.

They immediately tied Pinocchio's arms behind him, slipped a rope around his neck, and hung him from the branch of a tree called the Big Oak.

They then sat down on the ground and waited. But after three hours, the puppet's eyes were still open, his mouth closed, and he was kicking more than ever.

Losing patience, the assassins said to Pinocchio, "Good-bye 'til tomorrow. Let's hope that when we come back you will be polite enough to be found quite dead, and with your mouth wide open."

And off they walked.

In the meantime, a wild northerly wind began to blow, and it beat the poor puppet from side to side, making him swing violently like the clapper of a bell.

The swinging was very painful and as the rope tightened he became more and more breathless.

Pinocchio's eyes dimmed and he was quite sure that he would die soon, but he continued to hope that some kind person would help him before it was too late. But when no one came, he remembered his poor father, and thinking he was dying, he stammered, "Oh, Father! Father! If only you were here!"

His breath failed him, and he was silent. He shut his eyes, opened his mouth, stretched his legs, gave a long shudder, and hung stiff.

{ Chapter 16 }

The beautiful child with blue hair

 hile poor Pinocchio hung from a branch of the Big Oak, more dead than alive, the beautiful child with the blue hair came to the window. When she saw the puppet hanging by his neck, and dancing up and down in the wind, she was overcome with compassion. She quietly clapped her hands three times and a large falcon flew to the windowsill.

"What are your orders, gracious fairy?" he asked, bowing his beak in reverence to her — for the child with the blue hair was in fact a beautiful fairy who had lived in the woods for over a thousand years.

"Do you see that puppet dangling from a branch of the Big Oak?"

"I see him."

"Fly there at once. With your strong beak, break the knot that keeps him hanging there, and then lie him gently on the ground at the foot of the tree."

The falcon flew away, and after two minutes he returned, saying, "I have done as you commanded."

"And is he alive or dead?"

"He looked dead, but he can't be, because as soon as I loosened the rope around his throat he muttered faintly, 'Now I feel better!'"

The fairy clapped her hands twice, and a magnificent poodle appeared, walking upright on his hind legs, like a man.

He was dressed as a coachman. He wore a three-cornered cap braided with gold, a curly white shoulder-length wig, and a chocolate-coloured waistcoat with diamond buttons and two big pockets to hold the bones that his mistress gave him at dinner. He also wore crimson velvet breeches, silk stockings, short boots, and a kind of umbrella case made of blue satin, in which to put his tail when the weather was stormy.

"Be quick, Medoro, like a good dog!" said the fairy to the poodle. "Get the most beautiful carriage in my coach house ready and go to the woods. When you come to the Big Oak, you'll find a poor puppet stretched out on the ground half dead. Pick him up and put him in the carriage. Bring him here to me. Have you understood?"

The poodle, to show that he had understood, shook the blue satin case on his tail three or four times and ran off as fast as a racehorse.

Shortly afterwards, a beautiful little carriage came out of the coach house. Its cushions were stuffed with canary feathers, and the inside was lined with

whipped cream, custard and sweet biscuits. The carriage was drawn by a hundred pairs of white mice, and the poodle, seated on the coach box, cracked his whip from side to side like a driver afraid of being late.

Less than a quarter of an hour later, the carriage came back. The fairy, who was waiting at the door, took the poor puppet in her arms and carried him to a small room that was lined with mother-of-pearl. Then she sent for the most famous doctors in the area.

The doctors came immediately, one after the other: the first a crow, the second an owl, and the third a talking grasshopper.

"I wish to know from you gentlemen," said the fairy, turning to the three doctors assembled round Pinocchio's bed, "if this unfortunate puppet is alive or dead!"

The crow, coming forward first, felt Pinocchio's pulse, his nose, and the little toe of his foot. Having done this, he solemnly declared, "In my opinion, the puppet is already quite dead. But if, unfortunately, he should not be dead, then it would be a sure sign that he is still alive!"

"I regret," said the owl, "that I must contradict my illustrious friend and colleague, the crow. In my opinion, the puppet is still alive. If, unfortunately, he should not be alive, then it would be a sure sign that he is dead!"

"And you, have you nothing to say?" the fairy asked the talking grasshopper.

"In my opinion, the best thing a wise doctor can do, when he doesn't know what he is talking about, is to be silent. Furthermore, I know this puppet. I have known him for some time!"

Just then Pinocchio was seized with a fit of convulsive trembling that shook the whole bed.

"That puppet there," continued the talking grasshopper, "is a perfect rogue."

Pinocchio opened his eyes, but shut them again quickly.

"He is a beggar, a layabout and a drifter."

Pinocchio hid his face beneath the sheets.

"That puppet there is a disobedient son whose poor father will die of a broken heart!"

Then, in the room, they all heard the muffled sounds of sobbing and crying. They were surprised to discover, when the sheets were lifted a little, that the sounds came from Pinocchio.

"When a dead person cries, it's a sign that he is on the road to getting well," said the crow solemnly.

"I am sorry to contradict my illustrious friend and colleague," added the owl, "but in my opinion, when a live person cries, it's a sign that he does not want to die."

{ Chapter 17 }

Pinocchio eats some sugar and tells a lie

s soon as the three doctors had left the room, the fairy put her hand to Pinocchio's forehead and realized that he had a dangerous fever.

She dissolved some white powder in half a glass of water and offered it to the puppet, saying gently, "Drink it, and in a few days you will be better."

Pinocchio looked at the glass, made a sour face, and asked in a whining voice, "Is it sweet or bitter?"

"It's bitter, but it will do you good."

"If it's bitter, I won't drink it."

"Listen to me, and drink it."

"I don't like anything bitter."

"Drink it, and when you have, I'll give you a lump of sugar to take away the taste."

"Where is the lump of sugar?"

"Here," said the fairy, taking a piece from a gold sugar bowl.

"Give me the lump of sugar first, and then I'll drink that bad, bitter water."

"Do you promise?"

"Yes."

The fairy gave him the sugar, and Pinocchio, having chewed and swallowed it instantly, said, "It would be a fine thing if sugar was medicine! I'd take it every day."

"Now keep your promise and drink these few drops of water, which will restore your health."

Pinocchio unwillingly took the glass and sniffed it. He put the glass to his lips. Then sniffed it again, and at last said, "It's too bitter! Too bitter! I can't drink it."

"How do you know that, when you haven't even tasted it?"

"I can imagine it! I know it from the smell. I want another lump of sugar, and then I'll drink it."

With all the patience of a good mother, the fairy put another lump of sugar in his mouth, and again handed him the glass.

"I can't drink it like this!" said the puppet.

"Why?"

"Because that pillow on my feet bothers me."

The fairy removed the pillow.

"It's useless. I still can't drink it."

"What's wrong now?"

"The door is half open. That bothers me."

The fairy closed the door.

"The fact is," cried Pinocchio, bursting into tears, "I won't drink that bitter water — no, no, no!"

"You'll be sorry, my boy."

"I don't care."

"Your illness is serious."

"I don't care."

"The fever will kill you in a few hours."

"I don't care."

"Aren't you afraid to die?"

"I'm not afraid in the least! I'd rather die than drink that bitter medicine."

At that moment, the door of the room flew open, and four black rabbits walked in, carrying a small coffin on their shoulders.

"What do you want with me?" cried Pinocchio, sitting up in terror.

"We've come to take you," said the biggest rabbit.

"To take me? But I'm not dead yet!"

"No, not yet. But you have only a few minutes to live, as you have refused the medicine that would cure you."

"Oh, fairy, fairy!" the puppet cried. "Give me the glass at once! And be quick, for pity's sake! I don't want to die! No, I will not die!"

He took the glass in both hands and emptied it in one gulp.

"We must have patience!" said the rabbits. "This time we've made our journey in vain." And lifting the coffin back onto their shoulders, they left the room, grumbling and murmuring.

A few minutes later, Pinocchio jumped down from the bed quite well. Wooden puppets are lucky enough to be seldom ill and quickly cured.

When the fairy saw him rushing around the room as happy and lively as a young cockerel, she said, "Then my medicine has really done you good?"

"Good? I should think so! It has restored me to life!"

"Then why on earth did you need so much persuasion to take it?"

"Because we boys are all like that! We're more afraid of the medicine than of the illness."

"Disgraceful! Children ought to know that a good remedy taken in time may save them from a serious illness, and perhaps even death."

"Oh, but next time I won't require so much persuasion. I'll remember those black rabbits with the coffin on their shoulders. And then I'll immediately take the glass in my hand, and down it will go!"

"Now, come here, and tell me how it came to be that you fell into the hands of those assassins."

"It started when the Showman, Fire-Eater, gave me some gold pieces and said, 'Go, and take them to your father!' but I met a fox and a cat on the road, two very respectable creatures, who said to me, 'Would you like those pieces of gold to become a thousand or two? Come with us, and we'll take you to the Field of Miracles,' and I agreed. And they suggested that we stop at the Lobster Inn first, eat, and leave together at midnight. When I woke up, they had already left, so I set off as well. You can't imagine how dark it was! On the road, I met two assassins dressed in coal sacks who said, 'Out with your money,' and I said, 'I have none,' because I had hidden the four gold pieces under my tongue. One of them tried to put his hand in my mouth, and I bit it off and spat it out, but instead of a hand, I spat out a cat's paw. I ran, but the assassins ran after me until they finally caught me, and tied me by the neck to a tree in these woods, and said, 'Tomorrow we will return, and then you'll be dead, with your mouth open, and we'll be able to carry off the pieces of gold that you've hidden under your tongue.'"

"And the four pieces — where have you put them?" asked the fairy.

"I've lost them!" said Pinocchio. But he was telling a lie — they were in his pocket.

As soon as he told the lie, his nose, which was already long, grew even longer.

"And where did you lose them?"

"In the woods near here."

At this second lie, his nose grew longer still.

"If you've lost them in the woods near here," said the fairy, "we'll look for them, and we'll find them, because everything that is lost in that wood is always found."

"Ah! Now I remember," replied the puppet. "I didn't lose the four gold pieces. I swallowed them by mistake while I was drinking your medicine."

At this third lie, his nose grew to such an extraordinary length that poor Pinocchio could not move in any direction. If he turned to one side, he hit his nose against the bed or the windowsill. If he turned to the other, he hit it against the wall or the door. If he lifted his head, he ran the risk of poking it in the fairy's eyes.

The fairy looked at him and laughed.

"What are you laughing at?" asked the puppet, very confused and worried about his nose.

"I'm laughing at the lies you've told."

"How can you possibly know that I've been telling lies?"

"Lies, my dear boy, are found out immediately, because they are of two sorts.

There are lies that have short legs, and lies that have long noses. Your lies, as it happens, have long noses."

Pinocchio, feeling very ashamed, tried to run out of the room; but he failed because his nose had grown so long that it no longer fitted through the door.

{ Chapter 18 }

The Field of Miracles

he fairy allowed the puppet to cry for a good half an hour over his nose. She did this to teach him a lesson and to stop him from telling lies — the most disgraceful habit that a child can have. But she was filled with compassion when she saw his swollen eyes and she clapped her hands. At that signal a thousand woodpeckers flew in the window. They perched on Pinocchio's nose and began to peck at it and in a few minutes his enormous and ridiculous nose was back to its usual size.

"What a good fairy you are," said Pinocchio, "and how much I love you!"

"I love you, too," answered the fairy, "and if you want to stay with me, you'll be my little brother, and I'll be your good sister."

"I would stay willingly, but what about my poor father?"

"I've thought of that, and your father already knows everything. He will be here tonight."

"Really?" shouted Pinocchio, jumping for joy. "I would like to go and meet him, with your permission. That poor old man has suffered so much because of me — I just want to give him a kiss."

"Go, then, but be careful not to get lost. Take the road through the woods, and I'm sure that you will meet him."

Pinocchio left and began to run like a deer as soon as he was in the woods. But as he approached the Big Oak, he heard people in the bushes, so he stopped. It was his two travelling companions, the fox and the cat, with whom he had eaten dinner at the Lobster Inn.

"Here is our dear Pinocchio!" cried the fox, kissing and hugging him. "What brings you here?"

"What brings you here?" repeated the cat.

"It's a long story," answered the puppet, "which I'll tell you when I have time. But you should know that the other night, when you left me alone at the inn, I met assassins on the road."

"Assassins! Oh, poor Pinocchio! And what did they want?"

"They wanted to rob me of my gold pieces."

"Villains!" said the fox.

"Infamous villains!" repeated the cat.

"But I ran away from them," continued the puppet, "and they followed me, and eventually caught me and hung me from a branch of that oak tree."

"How dreadful!" said the fox. "What a world we live in! Where can respectable people like us be safe?"

While they were talking, Pinocchio noticed that the cat had lost her right front paw. "What's happened to your paw?"

The cat tried to answer but became confused. So the fox immediately interrupted, "My friend is too modest, and that's why she doesn't speak. I'll answer for her. I must tell you that an hour ago we met an old wolf on the road, who was almost fainting from hunger. He asked us for food, but not having so much as a fishbone to give him, my friend, who has the heart of a saint, bit off one of her front paws and threw it to the poor wolf so he might eat it."

As he said this, the fox wiped away a tear.

Pinocchio was also touched and said to the cat, "If all cats were as kind as you, how lucky the mice would be!"

"And what are you doing here?" the fox asked Pinocchio.

"I'm waiting for my father, who will be here any minute."

"And your gold pieces?"

"I have them in my pocket – except the one that I spent at the Lobster Inn."

"And to think that those four pieces might become one or two thousand by tomorrow! Why don't you listen to my advice? Why not go and bury them in the Field of Miracles?"

"It's impossible today. I'll go another day."

"Another day will be too late!" said the fox.

"Why?"

"Because the field has been bought by a gentleman, and after tomorrow no one will be allowed to bury money there."

"How far away is the Field of Miracles?"

"Not even two miles. Will you come with us? In half an hour you'll be there. You can bury your money, and in a few minutes you'll collect two thousand coins, and this evening you'll return with your pockets full. Will you come?"

Pinocchio thought of the good fairy, Geppetto, and the warning of the talking grasshopper, and he hesitated before answering. In the end, however, he did as all boys who have no sense and no heart do, he nodded and said to the fox and the cat, "Let's go! I'll come with you."

So off they went.

After having walked half the day, they reached a town called Fools' Trap. As soon as Pinocchio entered the town, he saw that the streets were crowded with dogs who had lost their coats and were yawning from hunger; shorn sheep, trembling with cold; cockerels without combs or crests who were begging for a grain of corn; large butterflies who could no longer fly because they had sold their beautifully-coloured wings; peacocks who had no tails and were ashamed to be seen; and pheasants who went scratching about, mourning their brilliant gold and silver feathers, gone for ever.

In the middle of this crowd of beggars, a fine carriage passed from time to time, carrying a fox, or a thieving magpie, or some other ravenous bird of prey.

"And where is the Field of Miracles?" asked Pinocchio.

"Right here, just a few steps away from us."

They walked through the town and came to a solitary field that looked just like any other field.

"Here we are," said the fox. "Now, dig a little hole in the ground with your hands and put your gold pieces into it."

Pinocchio dug a hole, put the four gold pieces into it, and filled it up with soil.

"Now, then," said the fox, "go to that canal over there, fetch a bucket of water, and water the ground where you have sowed your gold."

Pinocchio went to the canal, but since he had no bucket, he took off one of his old shoes, filled it with water, and then watered the ground over his gold pieces.

"Is there anything else to be done?" the puppet asked.

"Nothing else," answered the fox. "We can go away now. You can come back in about twenty minutes, and you'll find a bush already growing, with its branches quite loaded with money."

Beside himself with joy, Pinocchio thanked the fox and the cat, and promised them a beautiful present.

"We wish for no presents," they answered. "It is enough for us to have taught you the way to get rich without hard work. That makes us very happy."

Having said this, they said goodbye to Pinocchio, wished him a good harvest, and left.

{ Chapter 19 }

Pinocchio is robbed

Pinocchio went back to the town and started to count the minutes one by one. And when he thought that it must be time, he ran back to the Field of Miracles.

He ran as fast as he could, his heart beating like a clock — *tick, tock, tick, tock*. All the time he was thinking, "What if instead of a thousand gold pieces, I find two thousand on the branches of the tree? Or instead of two thousand, suppose I find five thousand? Or instead of five thousand, what if I find a hundred thousand? Oh! What a fine gentleman I would become! I would have a beautiful palace, a thousand little wooden horses and a thousand stables to amuse myself with, a cellar full of sweet syrups, and a library full of sweets, tarts, plum cakes, macaroons, and biscuits with cream."

While he was imagining these things, he got closer to the field and stopped to see whether he could see a tree laden with money, but he saw nothing. He went another thirty steps — nothing. He entered the field and went right up to the little hole where he had buried his gold pieces — nothing. He took his hands out of his pockets and scratched his head.

Suddenly, he heard an explosion of laughter nearby. Looking up he saw a large parrot perched on a tree, pruning the few feathers he had left.

"Why are you laughing?" asked Pinocchio angrily.

"I'm laughing because while pruning my feathers, I tickled myself under my wings."

The puppet did not answer. He went to the canal, filled the same old shoe full of water, and again watered the earth that covered his gold pieces.

While he was doing this he heard another laugh, more impertinent than the first.

"Once and for all," shouted Pinocchio crossly, "tell me, you ill-educated parrot, what are you laughing at?"

"I'm laughing at simpletons who believe in all the foolish things they hear, and who allow themselves to be tricked by those more cunning than they are."

"Are you, perhaps, speaking of me?"

"Yes, I'm speaking of you, poor Pinocchio — of you who are simple enough to believe that money can be sown and gathered in fields. I also believed it once, and am now suffering because of it. I have finally learned that to put a few pennies together honestly, one must know how to earn them, either by physical work or the cleverness of your own brain."

"I don't understand," said the puppet, who was already trembling with fear.

"Have patience! I'll explain myself better," said the parrot. "You must know that while you were in town, the fox and the cat returned to the field. They took the buried money and then fled. And no one will be able to catch them now."

Pinocchio stood with his mouth open and, choosing not to believe the parrot's words, began to dig up the earth he had watered. He dug and dug and dug, but the money was no longer there.

He rushed back to the town and went straight to the Court of Justice to denounce the two thieves who had robbed him.

The judge was an old gorilla whose age, white beard and gold spectacles made him look most respectable. His spectacles had no lenses, but he wore them because of an inflammation of the eyes that had tormented him for years.

Pinocchio told the judge all the particulars of the infamous fraud. He gave the names, surnames, and other details of the two rascals, and ended by demanding justice.

The judge listened with great kindness and interest, and was very moved by the story. And when Pinocchio had finished, the judge stretched out his hand and rang a bell.

At this summons, two mastiffs, dressed as policemen, immediately appeared. Pointing to Pinocchio, the judge said to them, "This poor devil has been robbed of four gold pieces. Arrest him and put him in prison immediately."

The puppet was petrified when he heard this unexpected sentence and tried to protest, but the policemen clamped his mouth shut and carried him off to prison.

He stayed in prison for four long months, and he would have stayed there longer but for an unexpected stroke of luck. The young emperor of Fools' Trap, having won a splendid victory over his enemies, ordered a public celebration. There were fireworks, horse races, and bicycle races, and he ordered that the prisons be opened and all the inmates set free.

"If the others are to be let out of prison, I ought to be let out, too," said Pinocchio to the jailer.

"No, not you," said the jailer, "because you don't belong to that class of people."

"I beg your pardon," replied Pinocchio. "I'm a criminal, too!"

"In that case, you're perfectly right," said the jailer, and taking off his hat and bowing to Pinocchio respectfully, he opened the prison door and let the puppet go.

{ Chapter 20 }

Pinocchio sets out for the fairy's house

inocchio was so happy to be free. He immediately left the town and set off for the fairy's house.

Rainy weather had turned the road into a marsh which the puppet sank into right up to his knees. But he would not give up. Spurred on by the desire to see his father and his blue-haired sister, he ran and leaped like a greyhound, and as he ran, he was splashed with mud from head to foot. As he went along he said to himself, "How many bad things have happened to me — and I have deserved them! I'm an obstinate, wilful puppet. I always want my own way. I do not listen to those who wish me well, and who have so much more sense than I do! But from now on, I'm determined to change and to become orderly and obedient. I've finally realized that disobedient boys come to no good and gain nothing. But will my father have waited for me? Will he be at the fairy's house? Poor man, it's so long since I last saw him. I'm dying to give him a hug and a kiss! And will the fairy forgive me for disobeying her? She was so kind and loving — I'm alive because of her! It would be hard to find a more heartless and ungrateful boy than me."

As he said this, he stopped suddenly, frightened to death, and took four steps backwards.

What had he seen?

He had seen an immense serpent stretched across the road. Its skin was green, its eyes were red, and its pointed tail smoked like a chimney.

Pinocchio was terrified. He walked away to a safe distance, sat down and waited for the serpent to go about its business and leave the road clear.

He waited and waited but the serpent did not move. Even from a distance Pinocchio could see the red light of its fiery eyes and the column of smoke rising from the end of its tail.

Trying to be brave, Pinocchio approached the serpent and said in a little, soft voice, "Excuse me, Mr Serpent, but would you be so good as to move a little to one side, just enough to allow me to pass?"

He might as well have spoken to a wall. The serpent did not move.

He began again in the same soft voice, "Mr Serpent, I'm on my way home and my father is waiting for me. It's such a long time since I last saw him! Please let me carry on my journey."

He waited for some sign in answer to this request, but there was none. In fact, the serpent, who had been sprightly and full of life, became completely still. It shut its eyes, and its tail stopped smoking.

"Can it really be dead?" asked Pinocchio, rubbing his hands with delight. But just as he was going to leap over it, the serpent suddenly rose up, and the puppet, in his terror, drew back, tripped and fell over.

He fell so awkwardly that his head stuck in the mud, leaving his legs waving in the air.

The serpent burst into a fit of laughter at the sight of the puppet with his head in the mud and legs in the air, kicking violently. It laughed, and laughed, and laughed, until it broke a blood vessel and died. And this time, it really was dead.

Pinocchio set off running in the hope that he would reach the fairy's house before dark. But soon he was so hungry that he could not bear it, so he jumped into a field with the intention of picking some grapes. If only he had not done that!

Pinocchio had barely reached the vines when – *crack!* – his legs were caught between two sets of sharp iron teeth. The pain was terrible. The poor puppet had been caught in a trap that had been put there to catch some big weasels who had been terrorizing the chicken yards in the area.

{ Chapter 21 }

The peasant and his guard dog

inocchio began to cry and scream. But his tears and groans were useless. There was not a house to be seen, and not a single person came down the road.

At last night came.

Partly from the pain of the trap that cut his legs, and partly from fear at realizing he was alone in the dark fields, the puppet was close to fainting. Just then, a firefly flew over his head. He called to it and asked, "Oh, little firefly, will you have pity on me and free me?"

"Poor boy!" said the firefly, who stopped and looked at him kindly. "How did you get your legs caught in those sharp iron teeth?"

"I came into the field to pick some grapes . . ."

"But were the grapes yours?"

"No."

"Then who taught you to take other people's property?"

"I was so hungry."

"Hunger, my boy, is not a good reason for taking what does not belong to you."

"That's true, that's true," said Pinocchio, crying. "I'll never do it again."

As they were talking, they were interrupted by the sound of someone approaching.

It was the owner of the field, tiptoeing to the trap to see whether it had caught one of the weasels during the night.

Imagine his surprise when he saw that he had caught a puppet instead of a weasel!

"Ah, little thief!" said the angry peasant. "So it's you who steals my chickens?"

"No, it's not me! It's not!" sobbed Pinocchio. "I only came into the field to pick some grapes!"

"He who steals grapes is quite capable of stealing chickens. I'll teach you a lesson that you won't forget quickly."

The man opened the trap, grabbed the puppet by the collar, and carried him to his house.

When he got to the yard in front of the house, he threw Pinocchio roughly on the ground, put his foot on the puppet's neck, and said, "It's late, and I want to go to bed. I'll deal with you tomorrow. In the meantime, since my guard dog died today, you can take his place. You will be my guard dog."

The peasant took a large collar covered with brass knobs, and strapped it tightly around the puppet's neck. A heavy chain was attached to the collar, which was then fastened to the wall.

"If it rains tonight," the man said, "you can go and lie down in the kennel. The straw that has been my poor dog's bed for the last four years is still there. Remember to keep your ears open. And if you hear the robbers, bark!"

After giving these instructions, the man went into the house, shut the door, and locked it.

Poor Pinocchio lay on the ground more dead than alive from cold, hunger and fear. From time to time he put his hands angrily to the collar that pinched his throat and cried, "It serves me right! It certainly serves me right! I was determined to be a drifter and a good-for-nothing. I listened to bad companions, and that's why I have always met with bad luck. If I had been a good little boy, if I had been willing to learn and to work, if I had stayed at home with my poor father, I would not be in this yard, working as a guard dog for a peasant. Oh, how I wish that I could be born again! But now it's too late, and I must have patience!"

After this outburst he felt better and went into the dog kennel and fell asleep.

{ Chapter 22 }

Pinocchio catches the thieves

H e had been fast asleep for about two hours when he was woken, at about midnight, by strange voices that seemed to come from the yard. He poked his nose out of the kennel and saw four small cat-like creatures with dark fur. But they were not cats; they were weasels — carnivorous little animals who are particularly fond of eggs and young chickens. One of the weasels, leaving his companions, came to the opening of the kennel and said in a low voice, "Good evening, Melampo."

"My name is not Melampo," answered the puppet.

"Oh! Then who are you?"

"I'm Pinocchio."

"And what are you doing here?"

"I'm acting as guard dog."

"But where is Melampo? Where is the old dog who lived in this kennel?"

"He died this morning."

"He's dead? Poor beast! He was so good. But judging by your face, I should say that you are also a good dog."

"Excuse me, but I'm not a dog."

"Not a dog? Then what are you?"

"I'm a puppet."

"And you're acting as guard dog?"

"Yes, as a punishment."

"Well, then, I'll offer you the same conditions that we made with the deceased Melampo, and I'm sure you will be satisfied with them."

"What are these conditions?"

"One night every week you will let us visit this yard and take eight chickens. Of these chickens, we will eat seven, and we'll give you one, on the understanding that you pretend to be asleep, and that you never bark or wake the peasant."

"Is that what Melampo did?" asked Pinocchio.

"Yes, and we were always on very good terms with him. Sleep quietly, and rest assured that before we go, we'll leave a beautiful plucked chicken by the kennel for your breakfast. Do we understand each other?"

"Only too clearly!" answered Pinocchio, but with a look that seemed to say, "We'll soon see about that!"

The four weasels, thinking they had a deal, crept to the chicken yard, opened the wooden gate with their teeth and claws, and slipped in one by one. But they had only just passed through when they heard the gate shut behind them with a loud bang.

It was Pinocchio who had shut it, and to keep it closed he put a big stone against the door.

He then began to bark, and he barked just like a guard dog: "Bow-wow! Bow-wow!"

When he heard the barking, the peasant jumped out of bed, grabbed his gun, came to the window and called, "What's the matter?"

"There are thieves!" answered Pinocchio.

"Where are they?"

"In the chicken yard."

"I'll come right down!"

The peasant was there almost immediately. He rushed into the yard, caught the weasels, put them in a sack, and said with great satisfaction, "I've got you at last! I should punish you, but I'm not that cruel. Instead, in the morning I will take you to the innkeeper in the next village, and he will skin and cook you like hares with a sweet and sour sauce. It's an honour you don't deserve, but I am a generous man and more than willing to do a good deed."

He then walked over to Pinocchio and asked, "How did you manage to catch them? To think that Melampo, my faithful Melampo, never found a thing!"

The puppet could have told him the whole story — of the disgraceful agreement that had been made between the dog and the weasels — but the dog was dead, and he thought to himself, "What good is it to accuse the dead? The dead are dead, and the best thing to be done is to leave them in peace!"

"When the thieves got into the yard," the peasant continued, "were you asleep or awake?"

"I was asleep," answered Pinocchio, "but the weasels woke me with their chatter, and one of them came to the kennel and said, 'If you promise not to bark and wake the master, we'll give you a fine, plucked chicken for your breakfast!' To think that they would have been bold enough to make such a proposal! Although I am a puppet, with many faults, there is one that I will never be guilty of, and that is dealing with, and sharing in the gains of, dishonest people!"

"Well said, my boy!" cried the peasant, slapping him on the shoulder. "Such sentiments do you honour, and as proof of my gratitude, I'll set you free at once. You may return home."

And he removed the dog collar.

{ Chapter 23 }

Pinocchio is left on his own

As soon as Pinocchio was released from the heavy and humiliating weight of the dog collar, he ran off across the fields and did not stop until he had reached the road that led to the fairy's house. When he reached it, he could see the woods where he had met the fox and the cat. He could also see the top of the Big Oak. But he could not see the little house belonging to the beautiful child with the blue hair.

He felt a terrible foreboding and began to run as fast as he could. He soon reached the field where the little white house had once stood. Instead of the house, there was a marble stone, on which were engraved these sad words:

Here lies
the child with the blue hair
who died from sorrow
because she was abandoned by
her little brother Pinocchio

I leave you to imagine the puppet's feelings when he had, with difficulty, read these words. He fell to the ground, covered the tombstone with kisses, and then burst into tears. He cried all night, and was still crying in the morning, even though he had no tears left. His heartbreaking sobs echoed around the surrounding hills.

As he wept, he said, "Oh, little fairy, why did you die? Why didn't I die – I who am so wicked – instead of you, who were so good? And my father? Where is he? Oh, little fairy, tell me where I can find him, for I want to stay with him always and never leave him again! Oh, little fairy, tell me that it's not true that you are dead! If you really love me, if you really love your little brother, come to life again. Come to life as you were before! Doesn't it make you sad to see me alone and abandoned? If assassins come, they will hang me again from the branch of a tree – and then I will certainly die. What can I do here, alone in the world? Now that I have lost you and my father, who will feed me? Where will I sleep? Who will make me clothes? It would be a hundred times better if I were to die too! Yes, I want to die! Boo-hoo-hoo!"

In this desperate state he tried to tear out his hair, but because his hair was made of wood, he could not even run his fingers through it.

Just then a large pigeon flew over his head, stopped, and called down to him, "Tell me, child, what are you doing there?"

"Can't you see? I'm crying!" said Pinocchio, lifting his head towards the voice and rubbing his eyes with his jacket.

"Tell me," continued the pigeon, "do you happen to know a puppet named Pinocchio?"

"Pinocchio? Did you say Pinocchio?" repeated the puppet, jumping quickly to his feet. "I'm Pinocchio!"

On hearing this answer, the pigeon flew quickly to the ground. He was bigger than a turkey.

"Do you also know Geppetto?" the bird asked.

"Do I know him? He is my poor father! Has he spoken to you about me? Will you take me to him? Is he still alive? Answer me, please! Is he still alive?"

"I left him three days ago on the seashore."

"What was he doing?"

"He was building a little boat for himself, to cross the ocean. For more than three months that poor man has been going all around the world looking for you. Having failed to find you, he has now decided to go to the new world to look for you."

"How far is it from here to the shore?" asked Pinocchio.

"More than six hundred miles."

"Six hundred miles! Oh, beautiful pigeon, what a fine thing it would be to have your wings!"

"If you want to go, I'll carry you there."

"How?"

"On my back. Do you weigh much?"

"I weigh next to nothing. I am as light as a feather."

Pinocchio jumped on the pigeon's back, putting a leg on each side of the bird as if on horseback. "Gallop, gallop, my little horse," he cried joyfully, "I'm keen to get there quickly!"

The pigeon took off, and in a few minutes he had flown so high that they almost touched the clouds. Finding himself at such an incredible height, the puppet was curious to turn and look down, but this made him dizzy, and he became so frightened that to stop himself from falling, he wound his arms tightly around the pigeon's neck.

They flew all day. Towards evening the pigeon said, "I'm very thirsty!"

"And I'm very hungry!" said Pinocchio.

"Let's stop at that pigeon house for a few minutes, and then we'll carry on so that we can get to the seashore by dawn."

They went into the deserted pigeon house and found nothing but a basin full of water and a basket of peas.

The puppet had never liked peas. He claimed they made him sick, but that evening he ate 'til he was full, and when he had nearly finished all the peas, he turned to the pigeon and said, "I never would have believed that peas were so good!"

"Ah, yes, my boy," replied the pigeon, "when hunger is real, and there is nothing else to eat, even peas taste delicious. Hunger makes no distinction between good and bad food."

After their little meal, they continued their journey. The following morning,

they reached the seashore.

The pigeon placed Pinocchio on the ground and, not wishing to be troubled with thanks for having done a good deed, flew quickly away.

The shore was crowded with people who were looking out to sea, shouting and pointing.

"What has happened?" Pinocchio asked an old woman.

"A poor father who has lost his son has gone away in a boat to look for him on the other side of the sea. But today the sea is so rough that the little boat is in danger of sinking!"

"Where is the little boat?"

"Out there, in line with my finger," said the old woman, pointing to what looked like a nutshell with a very small man in it.

Pinocchio fixed his eyes on it and then let out a piercing scream, crying, "It's my father! It's my father!"

Beaten by the fury of the waves, the boat disappeared for a moment in the trough of the sea, and then reappeared. Pinocchio, standing on top of a high rock, kept calling his father's name, and signalling to him with his hands, his handkerchief, and his cap.

And although he was miles away, Geppetto seemed to recognize his son. He also took off his cap and waved it, and tried to make Pinocchio understand that he would have returned if he could have, but the sea was so rough that he could not get back to the shore.

Suddenly, a huge wave swept over the boat. The people waited, hoping the little boat would reappear, but it did not.

"Poor man!" said the fishermen who were gathered on the shore. They murmured a prayer and then turned to go.

But just then they heard a desperate cry. Looking back, they saw a little boy jump from a rock into the sea, yelling, "I'll save my father!"

Being made of wood, Pinocchio floated easily, and he swam like a fish. One moment they saw him disappear under the water, carried down by the fury of the waves, and the next they could see an arm or a leg. At last they lost sight of him, and did not see him again.

"Poor boy!" said the fishermen. They murmured another prayer and then returned home.

{ Chapter 24 }

The Island of the Busy Bees

inocchio swam all night in the hope that he would be in time to save his father. And what a horrible night it was! There was hail and rain and thunder and lightning.

Towards morning he saw a long strip of land not far off. It was an island in the middle of the sea.

He tried his best to reach the shore, but it was impossible. The waves knocked him about as if he was a stick or a wisp of straw, until a huge wave rolled in and he was lifted up and thrown violently onto the sand.

He hit the ground with such force that his ribs and all his joints rattled, but he was consoled by his wonderful escape from the sea.

Eventually the sky cleared, the sun shone, and the sea became as quiet and smooth as oil.

The puppet spread his clothes to dry in the sun and began to look everywhere in the hope of seeing a little boat on the water with a little man in it. He looked and looked, but could only see the sky, the sea, and the sail of a ship that looked no bigger than a fly.

"If I only knew what this island was called!" he said. "If I only knew whether it was inhabited by civilized people — that is, by people who don't hang boys from the

branches of trees. But there is nobody to ask."

The idea of finding himself completely alone on this uninhabited island made him so sad that he was about to cry. But at that moment, he saw a big fish swimming by not far from the shore. It was going quietly about its own business, with its head out of the water.

Not knowing its name, the puppet called out in a loud voice, "Hello, Mr Fish! May I have a word with you?"

"Two if you like," answered the fish, who was a dolphin, and so polite that few like him are to be found in any sea in the world.

"Would you be kind enough to tell me if there are villages on this island where I could find something to eat, without running the risk of being eaten?"

"Certainly there are," replied the dolphin. "You'll find one very near here."

"And how do I get there?"

"Take the path to your left and follow your nose. You can't go wrong."

"Would you tell me something else? Since you swim in the sea all day and all night, have you by chance met a little boat with my father in it?"

"And who is your father?"

"He is the best father in the world — and it would be difficult to find a worse son than me."

"The little boat must have sunk during the terrible storm last night," answered the dolphin.

"And my father?"

"He must have been swallowed by the terrible shark that has been devastating our waters."

"Is this shark very big?" asked Pinocchio, who was already trembling with fear.

"Big?" replied the dolphin. "He is bigger than a five-storey house, and his mouth is so enormous and so deep that a steam train could easily pass down his throat."

"Mercy!" exclaimed the terrified puppet. Pinocchio put on his clothes as quickly as possible, thanked the dolphin and said goodbye.

He took the path that had been pointed out to him and began to walk so fast that he was almost running. He turned to look behind him at the slightest noise, terrified that the terrible shark with a steam train in its mouth might be chasing him.

After walking for half an hour, he reached a little village called The Village of the Busy Bees. The road was full of people running here and there on business. Everyone was working. Everyone had something to do. There was not a single idler or drifter anywhere.

"Ah!" said Pinocchio at once, "I see that this village will never suit me! I wasn't born to work!"

But by this time he was incredibly hungry, for he had not eaten anything for twenty-four hours — not even a few peas.

There were only two ways that he could get food — ask for work, or beg for a penny or a mouthful of bread.

He was ashamed to beg, for his father had always told him that no one had a right to beg except the old and the weak. The ones who deserve help and compassion are those who are no longer able to earn their own living, but it is the duty of everyone else to work. And if they will not work then it is their problem if they go hungry.

At that moment a man came down the road, tired and panting. He was dragging along two carts full of coal, but with great difficulty.

Pinocchio, judging by his face that he was a kind man, approached him, looked

down with shame, and said, "Would you give me a penny — I'm dying of hunger!"

"Not a penny," said the man, "but I'll pay you two pennies if you help me drag these two carts of coal home."

"I'm surprised by you!" answered the puppet. "I'm not used to doing the work of a donkey. I've never drawn a cart!"

"All right then," answered the man. "But, if you're really dying of hunger, eat two slices of your pride, and be careful not to get indigestion."

A few minutes later a mason walked down the road, carrying a basket of mortar on his shoulders.

"Good man, would you give a penny to a poor, hungry boy?"

"Willingly," answered the man. "Come with me and carry the mortar, and instead of a penny I'll give you five."

"But the mortar is heavy," objected Pinocchio, "and I don't want to tire myself."

"If you don't want to tire yourself, then, amuse yourself with your hunger."

In less than half an hour, twenty other people went by, and Pinocchio asked charity of them all, but they all answered, "Aren't you ashamed to beg? Instead of idling about the roads, go and look for a little work and learn to earn your bread."

At last a woman walked by, carrying two pitchers of water.

"Will you let me drink a little water from one of your pitchers?" asked Pinocchio, who was burning with thirst.

"Drink, if you wish!" said the woman, putting the two pitchers down.

Pinocchio drank like a fish, and as he dried his mouth he mumbled, "I've had enough to drink. If only I could eat as well!"

Hearing these words, the woman said, "If you'll help me carry these pitchers of water home, I'll give you a piece of bread."

Pinocchio looked at the pitcher and said nothing.

"And besides the bread you'll have a nice dish of cauliflower, dressed with oil and vinegar," added the good woman.

Pinocchio looked at the pitcher again and answered neither yes nor no.

"And after the cauliflower I'll give you some sweets."

This last temptation was so great that Pinocchio could not resist any longer. "Yes," he said, "I'll carry the pitcher to your house."

The pitcher was heavy, and the puppet, not being strong enough to carry it in his hands, had to carry it on his head.

When they reached the house, the woman made Pinocchio sit down at a small table, and she put bread, cauliflower, and sweets in front of him.

Pinocchio did not eat, he devoured. His stomach was like a house that had been left empty for five months.

When his hunger was somewhat appeased, he lifted his head to thank the woman. But as he looked at her, he groaned in astonishment. He stared at her with wide eyes, his fork in the air, and his mouth full of bread and cauliflower, as if bewitched.

"What has surprised you so much?" asked the woman, laughing.

"It's . . . it's . . . it's that you are like . . . that you remind me . . . yes, yes, yes, the same voice . . . the same eyes, the same hair . . . yes, yes, yes . . . you also have blue hair, like she did! Oh, little fairy! Tell me that it's you! Don't make me cry any more! If only you knew! I've cried so much. I've suffered so much!"

Having said this, Pinocchio threw himself at her feet, embraced the mysterious woman's knees, and began to cry bitterly.

{ Chapter 25 }

Pinocchio promises to be good and studious

At first the good woman insisted that she was not the little blue-haired fairy, but realizing that she had been found out, she confessed and said to Pinocchio, "You little rascal! How did you know who I was?"

"It was my great affection for you that told me."

"Do you remember? You left me when I was a child, and now I'm a woman — a woman almost old enough to be your mother."

"I'm very pleased, as now, instead of calling you my sister, I'll call you Mother. I've always wanted to have a mother like other boys have! But how did you manage to grow so fast?"

"That's a secret."

"Tell me, for I would also like to grow."

"But you can't grow," replied the fairy.

"Why?"

"Because puppets never grow. They are born puppets, they live puppets, and they die puppets."

"I'm sick of being a puppet!" cried Pinocchio, slapping himself on the head. "It's time that I became a man!"

"And you will become one, if you deserve it."

"Really? And what can I do to deserve it?"

"That's simple — learn to be a good boy."

"And you think I'm not?"

"You are quite the opposite. Good boys are obedient, and you . . ."

"And I never do what I'm told."

"Good boys like learning and working, and you . . ."

"And I lead a lazy idler's life."

"Good boys always tell the truth . . ."

"And I always tell lies."

"Good boys go to school willingly . . ."

"And school gives me pain all over my body. But starting today, I'll change."

"Do you promise?"

"I promise. I'll become a good boy, and I'll make my father proud. Where is my poor father?"

"I don't know."

"Will I ever see him again?"

"I think so. Yes, I am sure of it."

Hearing this answer, Pinocchio was so delighted that he took the fairy's hands and kissed them. "Tell me, Mother," he asked, looking at her lovingly, "wasn't it true that you were dead?"

"It seems not," said the fairy, smiling.

"If you only knew how sad I was when I read, 'Here lies . . .'"

"I know, and that's why I have forgiven you. I saw from the sincerity of your grief that you had a good heart; and when boys have good hearts, even if they are scamps and have bad habits, there's always the hope that they will turn to better ways. That's why I came to look for you. I will be your mother."

"Oh, how wonderful!" shouted Pinocchio, jumping for joy.

"You must obey me and do everything that I ask you to."

"Oh, I will!"

"Tomorrow," said the fairy, "you will start school."

Pinocchio immediately became a little less joyful.

"Then you must choose a profession or a trade."

Pinocchio became very downcast.

"What are you muttering?" asked the fairy sharply.

"I was saying," moaned the puppet, "that it seemed too late for me to go to school now."

"No, my boy. It's never too late to learn."

"But I don't want to learn a profession or a trade."

"Why?"

"Because working tires me out."

"My boy," said the fairy, "those who talk that way almost always end up either in prison or the hospital. Every man, whether he is born rich or poor must do something to occupy himself. Laziness is a dreadful illness and must be cured in childhood, for once we are old, it can never be cured."

Touched by these words, Pinocchio lifted his head quickly and said, "I'll study, I'll work, I'll do everything you tell me to. I am tired of being a puppet, and I want to become a boy. You promised me that I could, didn't you?"

"I did promise, and now it depends on you."

{ Chapter 26 }

Pinocchio goes to see the shark

The next day, Pinocchio went to school.

All the mischievous boys were delighted when they saw a puppet walk into their school. They laughed as though they would never stop. They played all sorts of jokes on him. One boy took off his cap, and another pulled his jacket. One tried to draw an ink moustache under his nose, and another tried to tie strings to his hands and feet to make him dance.

At first, Pinocchio pretended not to care. But he soon lost patience and, turning to those who were teasing and making fun of him the most, said, "Watch out, boys. I didn't come here to be your fool. I respect others, and I expect to be respected."

"Well said, clown! You've spoken like a book!" howled the boys, convulsing with laughter. One of them, even ruder than the others, stretched out his hand, intending to grab the puppet by the end of his nose. But he was not fast enough and Pinocchio kicked the boy's shins under the table.

"Ouch, what hard feet!" roared the boy, rubbing the bruise the puppet had given him.

"And what elbows! They're even harder than his feet!" said another, who had received a blow to the stomach for his rude jokes.

But the kick and the blow won Pinocchio the respect of the boys and they all made friends with him.

Even the schoolmaster praised him, for he found Pinocchio attentive, studious, and intelligent — always the first to arrive, and the last to leave when school was over.

But he had one fault: he made too many friends, and among them were several naughty boys who disliked studying.

The schoolmaster warned him every day, and the good fairy never failed to repeat it. "Be careful, Pinocchio!" she said. "Those bad classmates of yours will make you lose all love of study sooner or later, and they may even bring upon you bad luck."

"There's no chance of that!" answered the puppet, shrugging his shoulders and touching his forehead as if as to say, "I've got too much sense for that!"

But one day, on his way to school, Pinocchio met several of his usual companions, who asked, "Have you heard the great news?"

"No."

"In the sea near here a shark as big as a mountain has appeared."

"Really? Do you think it could be the same shark that was there when my poor father was drowned?"

"We're going to the shore to see him. Do you want to come?"

"No, I'm going to school."

"Who cares about school? We can go to school tomorrow. Whether we have a lesson more or a lesson less, we will always be the same dumb donkeys."

"But what will the schoolmaster say?"

"The schoolmaster may say what he likes. He's paid to grumble all day."

"And my mother?"

"Mothers know nothing," answered the bad little boys.

"I know what I'll do," said Pinocchio. "I have reasons for wanting to see the shark, but I'll go and see him after school."

"Poor donkey!" said one of the boys. "Do you think that a fish of that size will wait for you? As soon as he is tired of being here, he'll leave, and then it'll be too late."

"How long does it take to get from here to the shore?" asked the puppet.

"We can be there and back in an hour."

"Then away!" shouted Pinocchio. "And he who runs fastest is the best!"

At this, the boys, with their books under their arms, rushed off across the fields, and Pinocchio, who was always in the lead, seemed to have wings on his feet.

From time to time he turned to taunt his companions, who were some distance behind. He was delighted to see them covered in dust and panting for breath, with their tongues hanging out of their mouths. But the poor puppet had no idea what terrors and dreadful disasters were awaiting him.

{ Chapter 27 }

Pinocchio gets in a fight

When he arrived at the shore, Pinocchio looked out to sea, but he saw no shark. The sea was as smooth as a mirror.

"Where's the shark?" he asked, turning to his companions.

"He must have gone to breakfast," said one of them, laughing.

"Or he's taking a little nap," added another, laughing louder yet.

From their ridiculous answers and silly laughter Pinocchio worked out that his companions had been teasing him, and he said angrily, "What fun is there in tricking me with the story of the shark?"

"Oh, it was great fun!" answered the little rascals in chorus.

"And in what way?"

"In making you miss school, and persuading you to come with us. Aren't you ashamed of always being so punctual and so diligent with your school work? Aren't you ashamed of studying so hard?"

"What business is it of yours if I study hard?"

"It concerns us a great deal, because it makes us look bad in the eyes of the schoolmaster."

"Why?"

"Because boys who study make those like us, who have no desire to learn, seem worse. And we don't like it. We have our pride, too!"

"Then what must I do to please you?"

"You must follow our example and hate school, lessons, and the schoolmaster — our three greatest enemies."

"And if I want to continue my studies?"

"In that case we'll have nothing more to do with you, and at the first opportunity, we'll make you pay for it."

"Really," said the puppet, shaking his head, "you make me want to laugh."

"Careful, Pinocchio!" shouted the biggest of the boys. "We'll have none of your superior airs. Don't come here to crow over us! If you're not scared of us, we're not scared of you. Remember that you are one, and we are seven."

"Seven, like the seven deadly sins," said Pinocchio with a shout of laughter.

"Listen to him! He's insulted us all! He called us the seven deadly sins!"

"Pinocchio, say you're sorry!"

"Cuckoo!" sang the puppet, putting his forefinger to the end of his nose scoffingly.

"Pinocchio, you'll regret it!"

"Cuckoo!"

"We'll beat you like a donkey!"

"Cuckoo!"

"You'll go home with a broken nose!"

"Cuckoo!"

"I'll give you a cuckoo!" said the most courageous of the boys. "Take this to begin with, and keep it for your supper tonight!"

And with that, he hit Pinocchio on the head with his fist.

But the puppet, as was to be expected, immediately returned the blow, and the fight began.

Pinocchio defended himself heroically. He used his feet, which were made with the hardest wood, so effectively that he kept his enemies at bay. His feet left a bruise wherever they hit, and one that would not be easily forgotten.

The boys, furious at not being able to get close to the puppet, turned to other weapons. They started throwing their books at him — dictionaries, spelling books, geography books, and other textbooks. But Pinocchio was quick and sharp-eyed, and he always managed to duck in time so that the books passed over his head and fell into the sea.

The fish were very surprised! They arrived in shoals, thinking that the books were something to eat. But after tasting a page or two, they spat them out quickly and grimaced as if to say, "We're used to much better!"

The fight was becoming quite vicious when, suddenly, a big crab came out of the water. He climbed slowly onto the shore and called out, in a hoarse voice that sounded like a trombone with a bad cold, "Stop that, you young rascals! These fights among boys always end badly. Something will happen!"

Poor crab! He might as well have preached to the wind. Even Pinocchio turned around and said rudely, "Hold your tongue, you tiresome crab! You better suck some lozenges to cure that cold in your throat. Or even better, go to bed!"

Just then, the boys, who had no more books of their own to throw, saw Pinocchio's book bag lying on the ground and grabbed it.

Among the books was one bound in strong cardboard. It was called *A Treatise on Arithmetic*.

One of the boys seized the book, aimed at Pinocchio's head, and threw it as hard as he could. But instead of hitting the puppet, the book struck one of his companions on the head, who turned as white as a sheet and cried, "Oh, Mother, help me! I'm dying!" as he fell onto the sand. Thinking he was dead, the terrified boys ran away as fast as possible and were soon out of sight.

But Pinocchio stayed. Although he was more dead than alive from grief and fright, he soaked his handkerchief in the sea and began to bathe the temples of his poor schoolmate. "Eugene! My poor Eugene!" cried Pinocchio. "Open your eyes and look at me! Why don't you answer? I didn't do it. It wasn't me that hurt you! Believe me, it wasn't! Open your eyes, Eugene. If you keep your eyes shut, I'll die, too. Oh! What will I do? How will I ever return home? How will I ever be brave enough to go back to my mother? What will become of me? Where can I run away to? Oh! How much better it would have been, a thousand times better, if I had gone to school! Why did I listen to my companions? They have ruined me. The schoolmaster said to me, and my mother repeated it often, 'Beware of bad companions!' But I'm a stubborn, wilful fool. I let them talk, and then I always go my own way! And I have to suffer for it. Because of this, ever since I was born, I've never had a happy quarter of an hour. Oh! What will happen to me?"

Pinocchio sobbed, struck his head with his fists, and called out Eugene's name. Suddenly, he heard the sound of footsteps approaching.

He turned and saw two policemen.

"What are you doing there on the ground?" they asked Pinocchio.

"I'm helping my schoolmate."

"Has he been hurt?"

"So it seems."

"Hurt indeed!" said one of the policemen, stooping down and examining Eugene closely. "This boy has been wounded on the temple. Who did it?"

"Not me," stammered the puppet breathlessly.

"If it wasn't you, then who was it?"

"Not me," repeated Pinocchio.

"And what was he wounded with?"

"With this book." And the puppet picked up *A Treatise on Arithmetic* and showed it to the policeman.

"And to whom does this book belong?"

"To me."

"That's enough. We need nothing more. Get up and come with us at once."

"But I . . ."

"Come with us!"

"But I'm innocent."

"Come along with us!"

Before they left, the policemen called to some fishermen who were passing near the shore in their boat, and said to them, "Carry this wounded boy to your house and look after him. Tomorrow we'll come and see him."

They turned to Pinocchio, placed him between them, and said in commanding voices, "Forward! And step lively, or it will be the worse for you!"

Without waiting for them to repeat it, the puppet set out along the road leading to the village. He hardly knew where he was. He thought he must be dreaming, and what a dreadful dream it was! He was beside himself. His eyes saw double, his legs shook, his tongue stuck to the roof of his mouth, and he could not say a word. But, in the middle of his confusion, his heart was pierced by a cruel thorn — the thought that he would have to walk under the windows of the good fairy's house with the two policemen. He would rather have died.

They had just reached the village when a gust of wind blew Pinocchio's cap off his head.

"May I go and get my cap?" said the puppet to the policemen.

"Go, then. But be quick."

The puppet went and picked up his cap, but instead of putting it on his head, he took it between his teeth and ran as fast as he could towards the seashore.

The policemen, thinking it would be difficult to catch him, sent a large mastiff after him, one that had won first prize in all the dog races. Pinocchio ran, but the dog ran faster. People came to their windows and crowded into the street, anxious to see the end of the desperate race. But their curiosity was not satisfied, for Pinocchio and the dog raised such clouds of dust that quite soon there was nothing to be seen at all.

{ *Chapter 28* }

Pinocchio is in danger of being fried

There was a terrible moment in this desperate race when Pinocchio thought all was lost, for Alidoro, the mastiff, ran so fast that he nearly caught the puppet.

Pinocchio could hear the dreadful beast panting just inches behind him, and could even feel the dog's hot breath.

Fortunately, the shore was close, and the sea just a few steps further.

As soon as he reached the shore, the puppet made a huge leap — a frog could have done no better — and plunged into the sea.

Alidoro tried to stop, but he had built up such momentum that he went into the sea, too. The poor dog could not swim, and the more he struggled, the further he sank under the water.

When he rose to the surface again, his eyes rolled with terror, and he barked, "I'm drowning! I'm drowning!"

"Drown, then!" shouted Pinocchio from a distance.

"Help me, Pinocchio! Save me!"

On hearing that, the puppet, who had a genuinely kind heart, was moved. "If I save your life," he said, turning to the dog, "will you promise not to bother me further, and not to chase me?"

"I promise! I promise! Be quick, for pity's sake, for if you delay another minute I'll be dead!"

Pinocchio hesitated, but then he remembered his father's saying that a good deed is never forgotten. So, he swam to Alidoro, grabbed his tail with both hands, and brought him safe and sound onto the dry sand.

The poor dog could not stand. He had swallowed so much salt water that he had swelled up like a balloon. The puppet, however, not wanting to trust him completely, thought it better to jump back into the water. When he was some distance from the shore, he called out to the dog, "Goodbye, Alidoro! A good journey to you! And give my best to all at home!"

"Goodbye, Pinocchio," answered the dog. "Thank you for saving my life. You've done me a great service, and in this world what is given is returned. I won't forget it."

Pinocchio swam on, keeping near the shore. At last he thought he had reached a safe place. He spotted a kind of cave among the rocks from which a cloud of smoke was rising.

"There must be a fire in that cave," he said to himself. "I'll be able to dry and warm myself, and then? And then we'll see."

Having made this decision, he approached the rocks. But just as he was going to climb up, he felt something under the water that rose higher and higher and carried him right into the air. He tried to escape, but it was too late. To his great surprise he found himself inside a huge net, together with fish of every shape and size, who were flapping and struggling as if they had gone mad.

At that same moment, a fisherman came out of the cave. He was so ugly, so horribly ugly, that he looked like a sea monster. His head was covered with a thick bush of green grass, his skin was green, his eyes were green, and his long beard was green. He looked like an immense lizard standing on its hind legs.

When the fisherman had pulled his net out of the sea, he exclaimed with great satisfaction, "Thank Heaven! I'll have a splendid feast of fish today!"

"I am lucky not to be a fish!" said Pinocchio to himself.

The net full of fish was carried into the dark and smoky cave. In the middle of the cave was a large frying pan full of oil, producing a breathtakingly rank smell.

"Now we'll see what fish we have caught!" said the green fisherman, and putting an enormous and misshapen hand into the net, he pulled out a handful of mullet.

He smelled them and he threw them into the pan without water.

He repeated the same process many times. And as he drew out the fish, his mouth watered, and he said, chuckling to himself, "What good whiting! What exquisite sardines! These crabs will be excellent! What delicious little anchovies!"

The last to remain in the net was Pinocchio.

As soon as the fisherman had taken him out, he opened his big green eyes and cried, half-frightened, "What sort of fish is this? I don't remember eating fish like this before!"

He looked at the puppet again, examined him all over, and ended by saying, "I know! He must be a crayfish!"

Pinocchio, upset at being mistaken for a crayfish, said in an angry voice, "A crayfish! You take me for a crayfish? I'm a puppet."

"A puppet?" replied the fisherman. "To tell the truth, a puppet is quite a new fish to me. All the better! I will eat you with greater pleasure."

"Eat me? Don't you understand? I'm not a fish! Don't you hear that I talk and reason as you do?"

"That's quite true," said the fisherman, "and because I see that you are a fish that can speak and reason, I'll treat you with all the consideration you deserve."

"What kind of consideration?"

"In token of my friendship, I'll give you the choice of how you would like to be cooked. Would you like to be fried in the frying pan, or would you prefer to be stewed with tomato sauce?"

"To tell the truth," answered Pinocchio, "I'd prefer to be set free so that I can return home."

"You're joking! Do you think I would miss the opportunity to taste such a rare fish? It's not every day, I assure you, that a puppet fish is caught in these waters. Leave it to me. I'll fry you in the frying pan with the other fish, and you'll be quite satisfied. It's always better to be fried with company."

Pinocchio began to cry and scream and beg for mercy, sobbing, "If only I had gone to school! I listened to my companions, and now I'm paying for it! Boo-hoo-hoo!"

He wriggled like an eel, making great efforts to slip out of the clutches of the green fisherman. But it was useless. The fisherman took a long rope, bound Pinocchio's hands and feet as if he had been a sausage, and threw him into the pan with the other fish.

He fetched a wooden bowl full of flour and began to flour each fish in turn. And as soon as they were ready, he threw them into the frying pan.

The first to dance in the boiling oil were the poor whiting. The crabs followed, then the sardines, and then the anchovies. At last it was Pinocchio's turn. Seeing himself so near death — and such a horrible death — he trembled so violently that he was unable to even beg for mercy.

Pinocchio pleaded with his eyes, but the green fisherman, not caring in the least, plunged him five or six times in the flour, coating him from head to toe until he looked like he was made of plaster.

He then took Pinocchio by the head, and . . .

{ *Chapter 29* }

Pinocchio returns to the fairy

ust as the fisherman was about to throw Pinocchio into the frying pan, a large dog entered the cave, led there by the delicious smell of fried fish.

"Get out!" shouted the fisherman, holding the floured puppet in his hand.

But the poor dog, who was as hungry as a wolf, whined and wagged his tail as if to say, "Give me a mouthful of fish, and I'll leave you in peace."

"Get out, I tell you!" repeated the fisherman, and he stretched out his leg to give him a kick.

But the dog, who was ravenous, would not leave. He turned on the fisherman, growling and baring his teeth.

Just then a feeble little voice was heard in the cave crying, "Save me, Alidoro! If you don't save me, I'll be fried!"

The dog recognized Pinocchio's voice, and to his extreme surprise he discovered that it came from the floured bundle in the fisherman's hand.

The dog leaped, grabbed the bundle in his mouth, and, holding it gently between his teeth, rushed out of the cave.

The fisherman ran after them, furious at seeing a fish he was so eager to eat snatched from him, but after a few steps he had a fit of coughing and had to give up.

When he reached the path that led to the village, Alidoro stopped and put Pinocchio gently on the ground.

"Thank you so much!" said the puppet.

"There's no need," replied the dog. "You saved me, and I've now saved you. We must all help each other in this world."

"But what brought you to the cave?"

"I was lying on the shore more dead than alive, when the smell of fried fish wafted over, so I followed it. If I had arrived a second later . . ."

"Don't!" groaned Pinocchio, who was still shaking with fright. "Don't speak of it! If you had arrived a second later, I would by this time have been fried, eaten, and digested. Brrr! It makes me shudder just to think of it!"

Alidoro, laughing, extended his right paw to the puppet, who shook it heartily, and then they parted.

The dog took the road home, and Pinocchio, left alone, went to a nearby cottage and said to a little old man who was warming himself in the sun, "Tell me, good man, do you know anything of a boy called Eugene who was wounded in the head?"

"Some fishermen brought him here, and now . . ."

"And now he's dead!" interrupted Pinocchio.

"No, he's alive, and has returned home."

"Really? Really?" cried the puppet, dancing with delight. "Then he was not seriously wounded?"

"It might have been very serious, even fatal," answered the little old man, "for they threw a thick, cardboard-bound book."

"And who threw it at him?"

"One of his schoolmates, one named Pinocchio."

"And who is this Pinocchio?" asked the puppet, pretending not to know.

"They say that he's a bad boy, a vagabond, a good-for-nothing."

"Lies! All lies!"

"Do you know Pinocchio?"

"By sight!" answered the puppet.

"And what's your opinion of him?" asked the little man.

"He seems to me to be a very good boy, anxious to learn, and obedient and affectionate to his father and family."

While the puppet was firing off all these lies, he touched his nose and discovered that it had grown a few inches longer. Very much alarmed, he cried out, "Don't believe what I've been telling you! I know Pinocchio very well, and I can assure you that he is really a very bad boy, disobedient and idle, who instead of going to school runs off with his companions to amuse himself!"

As soon as he had spoken these words, his nose shrank back to its original size.

"And why are you so white?" asked the old man suddenly.

"Well, I wasn't watching where I was going, and I rubbed up against a wall that had just been whitewashed," answered the puppet, ashamed to confess that he had been floured like a fish prepared for the frying pan.

"And what have you done with your jacket, your trousers, and your cap?"

"I was robbed. Perhaps you could give me some clothes to go home in?"

"My boy, I have nothing but a little sack in which I keep beans. If you want it, take it. You are welcome to it."

Pinocchio did not wait to be told twice. He took the sack and cut a hole in the end and one in each side. He put it on like a shirt, and set off for the village.

But as he went, he began to feel very uncomfortable; for each step forward, he took another step backward, saying to himself, "How will I ever face my good little fairy? What will she say when she sees me? Will she forgive me a second time? I'm afraid that she won't! Oh, I'm sure that she won't! And it serves me right, for I'm a rascal. I'm always promising to better myself, and I never keep my word!"

It was night when Pinocchio reached the village. As a storm had come up, and it was raining very hard, he went straight to the fairy's house.

When he arrived, his courage failed him, and instead of knocking he ran away. He returned to the door a second time but could not make up his mind. He came back a

third time, and still he dared not knock. The fourth time he took hold of the knocker and, trembling, gave a little knock.

He waited and waited. At last, after half an hour, a window on the top floor opened – the house was four storeys high – and Pinocchio saw a big snail with a lighted candle on her head looking out. She called to him, "Who's there at this hour?"

"Is the fairy home?" asked the puppet.

"The fairy is asleep and must not be woken. But who are you?"

"It's me!"

"Who is me?"

"Pinocchio."

"And who is Pinocchio?"

"The puppet who lives in the fairy's house."

"Ah, I understand!" said the snail. "Wait for me there. I'll come down and open the door for you."

"Be quick, please, I'm dying of cold."

"My boy, I am a snail, and snails are never in a hurry."

An hour passed, and then two, and the door was still not opened. Pinocchio, who was soaked through and trembling

from cold and fear, knocked again, and this time he knocked louder.

At this second knock, a window on the third floor opened, and the same snail appeared.

"Beautiful little snail," cried Pinocchio from the street. "I've been waiting for two hours! And two hours on such a bad night seem longer than two years. Be quick, please!"

"My boy," answered the calm little snail, "I'm a snail, and snails are never in a hurry."

And the window was closed again.

Soon midnight struck, then one o'clock, then two o'clock, and still the door remained closed.

Pinocchio lost all patience and grabbed the knocker in a rage, intending to give a knock that would be heard throughout the house. But the knocker, which was iron, suddenly turned into an eel and slipped out of his hands, and disappeared into the stream of water that ran down the middle of the street.

"Oh-ho!" shouted Pinocchio, blind with rage. "Since the knocker has disappeared, I'll kick the door instead!"

And drawing back his foot, he gave the door an enormous kick. The blow was so violent that his foot went through the wood and got stuck; when he tried to pull it out, he couldn't. It remained fixed like a nail that has been hammered down.

Poor Pinocchio! He had to spend the rest of the night with one foot on the ground and the other in the air.

Finally, at dawn, the door was opened. The little snail had rushed to the door, taking only nine hours to come down from the fourth floor.

"What are you doing with your foot stuck in the door?" she asked the puppet, laughing.

"It was an accident. Do try, beautiful little snail, to free me from this torture."

"My boy, that's the work of a carpenter, and I have never been a carpenter."

"Beg the fairy for me!"

"The fairy is asleep and must not be woken."

"But what am I supposed to do all day, stuck in this door?"

"You can amuse yourself by counting the ants."

"At least bring me something to eat, for I'm terribly hungry."

"At once!" said the snail.

After three and a half hours, she came back carrying a silver tray on her head. On the tray was a loaf of bread, a roast chicken, and four ripe apricots.

"Here is the breakfast that the fairy has sent you," said the snail.

The puppet felt very comforted at the sight of these good things. But when he began to eat them, he was disgusted to find that the bread was made of plaster, the chicken was cardboard, and the four apricots were painted stones!

He wanted to cry. In his despair, he tried to throw away the tray, but instead, either from grief or exhaustion, he fainted.

When he came to, he found that he was lying on a sofa, with the fairy beside him.

"I'll forgive you once more," the fairy said. "But if you behave badly a third time, you are in trouble!"

Pinocchio promised, and he swore that he would study, and that in the future he would always behave well.

Pinocchio kept his word for the rest of the year. He became the best pupil at his school, and his behaviour was so good that the fairy was very pleased. One day she said to him, "Tomorrow your wish will be granted."

"Do you mean . . . ?"

"Tomorrow you'll cease to be a wooden puppet, and you'll become a real boy."

No one who had not seen it could ever imagine how happy Pinocchio was when he heard this long-awaited news. All his schoolmates were to be invited to a grand breakfast at the fairy's house the following day so that they could celebrate the great event. The fairy had prepared two hundred cups of coffee and milk, and four hundred bread rolls buttered on both sides. The day promised to be a happy one, but . . .

Unfortunately, in the lives of puppets, there is always a 'but' that spoils everything.

{ Chapter 30 }

Why there was no party

inocchio asked the fairy's permission to go around town and invite his friends to the party. The fairy let him go, but reminded him to be home before dark.

"I promise to be back in an hour," said the puppet.

"Be careful, Pinocchio! Children are always quick to make promises, but they are not so ready to keep them," answered the fairy.

"But I'm not like other children. When I say something, I do it."

"We'll see. If you are disobedient again, so much the worse for you."

"Why?"

"Because children who don't listen to the advice of those who know more than they do always meet with some misfortune or other."

"I've learned my lesson," said Pinocchio. "I'll never make that mistake again."

"We'll see if that is true."

Without saying another word, the puppet said goodbye to his good fairy, who was like a mother to him, and left the house singing and dancing.

In less than an hour, all his friends were invited. Some accepted at once. Others

hesitated at first, but agreed to come when they heard that the rolls would be buttered on both sides.

Among Pinocchio's friends and schoolmates, there was one that he liked best. This boy's name was Romeo, but he went by the nickname of Lampwick, because he was thin, straight, and bright, just like the new wick of a lamp.

Lampwick was the laziest, naughtiest boy in the school, but Pinocchio liked him all the same. In fact, he had gone to his house first to invite him to breakfast, but Lampwick was out. The puppet went back a second time, but he was still out. He went a third time and Lampwick was still not there. Pinocchio looked everywhere, and at last he saw him hiding in the porch of a peasant's cottage.

"What are you doing?" asked Pinocchio.

"I'm waiting for midnight, so I can leave."

"Why, where are you going?"

"Very, very far away."

"I've been to your house three times looking for you."

"What did you want with me?"

"Don't you know about the great event? Haven't you heard of my good luck?"

"What is it?"

"Tomorrow I will cease to be a puppet, and become a boy like you and all the other boys."

"Much good may it do you!"

"Tomorrow, therefore, I expect you to have breakfast at my house."

"But I told you that I'm going away tonight."

"At what time?"

"In a short time."

"And where are you going?"

"I'm going to live in a faraway country, the most wonderful country in the world. A real paradise!"

"What is it called?"

"It's called Playland. Why don't you come, too?"

"Me? No, never!"

"You're wrong, Pinocchio. Believe me, if you don't come you'll be sorry. Where else could you find a better country for us boys? There are no schools, no schoolmasters, and no books. In that wonderful land nobody ever studies. There's never school on Saturday, and every week consists of six Saturdays and one Sunday. Just think! Holiday starts on the first day of January and ends on the last day of December. That's the country for me! That's what all civilized countries should be like!"

"But what do people do in Playland?"

"They play and amuse themselves all day long. When night comes, you go to bed, and in the morning, you start all over again. What do you think of that?"

"Hmm!" said Pinocchio, shaking his head slightly as if to say, "That sort of life wouldn't be too bad!"

"Well, will you come with me? Yes or no? Make up your mind!"

"No. I promised my good fairy that I would become a good boy, and I'll keep my word. And the sun is setting, so I must go. Goodbye, and a good journey to you."

"Where are you rushing off to in such a hurry?"

"Home. My good fairy wants me to be back before dark."

"Wait another two minutes."

"I'll be late."

"Only two minutes."

"And if the fairy scolds me?"

"Let her scold. Once she has scolded, she will stop," said that rascal Lampwick.

"And how are you going? Alone or with companions?"

"Alone? There will be more than a hundred boys with me."

"Will you be going on foot?"

"A stagecoach will pass by shortly to take me to that happy country."

"What I would not give for the stagecoach to pass by now!"

"Why?"

"So I can see you all off together."

"Stay for a little bit longer, and you can do so."

"No, no, I must go home."

"Wait another two minutes."

"I've already delayed too long. The fairy will be worried about me."

"Poor fairy! Is she afraid that the bats will eat you?"

"But are you really sure that there are no schools in that country?" Pinocchio asked.

"Not a single one."

"And no schoolmasters either?"

"Not one."

"And no one ever has to study?"

"Never, never, never!"

"What a wonderful country!" said Pinocchio. "I've never been there, but I can imagine it."

"Why don't you come, too?"

"It's useless to tempt me. I promised my good fairy that I would become a sensible boy, and I won't break my word."

"Goodbye, then, and give my best to all the other boys at school, if you meet them in the street."

"Goodbye, Lampwick, have a good journey! Have a wonderful time, and think of your friends now and then."

On saying this, the puppet made two steps to go, but then he stopped, turned to his friend, and asked, "But are you quite sure that in that country all the weeks consist of six Saturdays and one Sunday?"

"Absolutely sure."

"Do you know for sure that holidays begin on the first day of January and end on the last day of December?"

"Quite sure."

"What a wonderful country!" repeated Pinocchio, looking enchanted. Then he added resolutely, "Goodbye for the last time, and have a good journey. When do you leave?"

"In just over an hour."

"What a pity! If it were only one hour, I would almost be tempted to wait."

"And the fairy?"

"It's already late. If I return home an hour later, it will be all the same."

"Poor Pinocchio! And if the fairy scolds you?"

"I'll let her scold. Once she has scolded, well, she'll stop."

In the meantime, it had become quite dark. Suddenly they saw a small light moving in the distance. They heard people talking and the sound of a trumpet, small and feeble like the hum of a mosquito.

"Here it is!" shouted Lampwick, jumping to his feet.

"What is it?" asked Pinocchio in a whisper.

"It's the stagecoach coming for me. Will you come, too? Yes or no?"

"But is it really true," asked the puppet, "that in that country children never have to study?"

"Never, never, never!"

"What a wonderful country! What a marvellous country!"

{ Chapter 31 }

The puppet sets out for Playland

t last the stagecoach arrived, and because its wheels were bound with rags, it was completely noiseless.

It was drawn by twelve pairs of donkeys, all the same size, but different colours. Some were grey, some were white, and some were spotted like pepper and salt. Others had large yellow and blue stripes.

But the most extraordinary thing was that the twelve pairs – that is, the twenty-four donkeys – had men's boots made of white leather on their hooves.

The coachman was a small man, broader than he was tall, soft and greasy like a lump of butter, with a round face like an orange, a little mouth that was always laughing, and a soft, caressing voice like that of a cat when it is miaowing to its mistress for some cream.

All the boys liked him as soon as they saw him. They hurried to find a place in his coach, keen to be taken to Playland, the true land of paradise.

The coach was quite full of boys between eight and twelve years old, packed in like herrings in a barrel. They were uncomfortable, squashed close together, and could hardly breathe, but nobody grumbled. The consolation of knowing that they would soon reach a country where there were no books, no schools, and no schoolmasters made them so happy that they did not feel tired, uncomfortable, hungry or thirsty.

As soon as the stagecoach stopped, the little man turned to Lampwick and, smirking and grimacing, said to him, "Tell me, my fine boy, would you like to go to that happy country?"

"I certainly would!"

"But I must tell you, my dear child, that there is no space in the coach. You can see for yourself that it's completely full."

"If there is no place inside," replied Lampwick, "I'll sit outside on the crossbar." And with a leap he seated himself astride the crossbar.

"And you, my love!" said the little man, turning in a flattering manner to Pinocchio. "What do you intend to do? Are you coming with us, or are you going to stay behind?"

"I'm going to stay behind," answered Pinocchio. "I'm going home. I intend to study and go to school, as all good children do."

"Much good may it do you!"

"Pinocchio," cried Lampwick, "listen to me. Come with us, and we'll have such fun."

"No, no, no!"

"Come with us, and we'll have such fun!" cried four other voices from inside the coach.

"Come with us, and we'll have such fun!" shouted a hundred voices in chorus from inside the coach.

"But if I come with you, what will my good fairy say?" said the puppet, who was beginning to give in to the pressure.

"Don't worry about that," said Lampwick. "Think only that we are going to a country where we'll be free to play all day."

Pinocchio did not answer. He just sighed. Then he sighed again. After sighing a third time, he said, "Make some room for me! I'm coming too!"

"The places are all full," replied the little man. "But to show you how happy I am that you're with us, you may have my seat on the box."

"And you?"

"Oh, I'll go on foot."

"No, I couldn't allow that. I would rather ride one of these donkeys," cried Pinocchio.

On saying this, he approached the right-hand donkey of the first pair and tried to climb onto it. But the donkey turned and kicked him in the stomach, sending him sprawling with his legs in the air.

All the boys roared with laughter.

But the little man did not laugh. He approached the rebellious donkey and, pretending to give it a kiss, bit off half its ear.

In the meantime, Pinocchio had picked himself up from the ground in a fury, and with a leap he seated himself on the poor animal's back. He leaped so splendidly that the boys stopped laughing and began to shout, "Hurrah, Pinocchio!" They clapped their hands and applauded as if they would never stop.

But the donkey suddenly kicked up its hind legs and threw Pinocchio into the middle of the road.

The roars of laughter started again, but the little man, instead of laughing, felt such affection for the unruly donkey that he kissed it again, and in doing so bit half of its other ear off. He then said to the puppet, "Mount him now without fear. That little donkey is very stubborn, but I whispered something into its ears which has, I hope, made him gentle and reasonable."

Pinocchio mounted, and the stagecoach started to move. While the donkeys were galloping and the coach was rattling over the stones of the road, the puppet thought he heard a low, quiet voice saying to him, "Poor fool! You've decided to do as you please, but you'll be sorry for it!"

Pinocchio was frightened and looked from side to side to see where the voice had come from, but he saw nobody. The donkeys galloped, the stagecoach rattled, the boys inside slept, Lampwick snored, and the little man seated on the box sang between his teeth:

> *"Everybody sleeps through the night,*
> *But I never sleep . . ."*

After they had gone another mile, Pinocchio heard the same voice saying to him, "Bear it in mind, you fool! Children who refuse to study, and turn their backs on books, schools, and schoolmasters, to spend their time having fun always come to a bad end. I know this from experience. A day will come when you'll weep as I am weeping now, but then it will be too late!"

On hearing these words whispered very softly, the puppet, more frightened than ever, jumped off the donkey and took hold of its bridle.

He was surprised to see that the donkey was crying, just like a boy!

"Excuse me, Mr Coachman," cried Pinocchio to the little man. "I've discovered an extraordinary thing! This donkey is crying."

"Let it cry. It will laugh when it gets some hay."

"Have you taught it to talk?"

"No, but it spent three years in the company of trained dogs, and it learned to mutter a few words."

"Poor beast!"

"Come, come," said the little man, "let's not waste time watching a donkey cry. Get back on and let's go. The night is cold, and the road is long."

Pinocchio obeyed without another word. At dawn, they arrived safely in Playland.

It was a country unlike any other country in the world. The population was made up entirely of children. The oldest were fourteen, and the youngest barely eight years old. In the streets there was such happiness, noise, and shouting, that it was enough to make a person's head spin. There were children everywhere. Some were playing with nuts, some with shuttlecocks, and some with balls. Some rode bicycles, while others

rode wooden horses. A group was playing hide and seek, and a few children were chasing each other. Some children were acting, some singing, some doing somersaults. Some were amusing themselves by walking on their hands, with their feet in the air. Others were spinning hoops, or strutting about dressed as generals, wearing leaf helmets and commanding a squadron of cardboard soldiers. Some were laughing, and some were shouting. Others clapped their hands, or whistled, or clucked like hens who had just laid an egg. There was so much noise that, without cotton wool in both ears, a person might have gone deaf. Here and there, canvas theatres had been put up, and they were crowded with children all day long. Inscriptions were written in charcoal on the walls of the houses: "Long live toys!" "No more schools!" "Down with arithmetic!" and other fine sentiments, all misspelled.

Pinocchio, Lampwick, and the other boys who had made the journey with the little man had barely set foot in the town before they became part of the crowd, making friends with everybody in just a few minutes. Where could happier or more contented children be found?

In the middle of continual games and every sort of amusement, the hours, days, and weeks passed like lightning.

"Oh, what a wonderful life!" said Pinocchio whenever he met Lampwick.

"See, then, wasn't I right?" replied Lampwick. "And to think that you didn't want to come! To think that you had intended to return home to your fairy, and to waste your time studying! If you are free today from the bother of books and school, you must admit that you owe it to me and my advice. Only a real friend would show such great kindness."

"It's true, Lampwick! If I'm now a happy boy, it is all your doing. And do you know what the schoolmaster used to say when he spoke of you? He always said to me, 'Don't have anything to do with that rascal Lampwick, he's bad company and will lead you astray!'"

"Poor schoolmaster!" replied Lampwick, shaking his head. "I know only too well that he disliked me and amused himself by speaking ill of me. But I'm generous, and I forgive him!"

"Noble soul!" said Pinocchio, hugging his friend and kissing him on the forehead.

This delightful life went on for five months, without a thought for books or school. Then, one morning, Pinocchio woke up to an unpleasant surprise that put him in a very bad mood.

{ Chapter 32 }

Pinocchio turns into a donkey, tail and all

 he surprise was that Pinocchio, when he woke up and scratched his head, discovered, to his great astonishment, that his ears had grown several inches!

He had always had very small ears, so small that they were invisible to the naked eye. So you can imagine how he felt when he found that his ears had become so long during the night that they were like two brooms.

He immediately went to find a mirror so that he could look at himself. Not being able to find one, he filled his wash bowl with water, looked into it, and saw a terrible reflection. He saw that he had grown a magnificent pair of donkey's ears!

Just think of poor Pinocchio's sorrow, shame, and despair!

He began to cry and howl, and beat his head against the wall. But the more he cried, the longer his ears grew. They grew and grew and became hairy at the tips.

At the sound of his loud cries, a beautiful little squirrel that lived on the first floor came into the room. Seeing the puppet in such grief, she asked, "What's the matter, my dear neighbour?"

"I'm ill, my dear little squirrel, very ill — and with an illness that frightens me. Do you know how to take a pulse?"

"I think so."

"Then feel, and see if I have a fever."

The little squirrel raised her right forepaw, felt Pinocchio's pulse, and then said with a sigh, "My friend, I'm sorry to give you bad news."

"What is it?"

"You have a very bad fever!"

"What kind of fever is it?"

"Donkey fever."

"That's a fever I don't understand," said the puppet, but he understood only too well.

"Then I'll explain it to you," said the squirrel, "for you must know that in two or three hours you will no longer be a puppet, or a boy."

"Then what will I be?"

"In two or three hours you will become a little donkey, like those that draw carts and carry cabbages and salad to market."

"Oh! Poor me! Poor me!" cried Pinocchio, grabbing his ears with his hands and pulling them furiously as if they belonged to somebody else.

"My dear boy," said the squirrel, trying to console him, "you can't do anything to stop it. It is destiny. It is written in the decrees of wisdom that all children who are lazy; who take a dislike to books, schools, and schoolmasters, and who pass their time in amusement and games must end up becoming little donkeys sooner or later."

"Is that really true?" sobbed the puppet.

"It's only too true, I'm afraid! And tears are now useless. You should have thought of that sooner!"

"But it wasn't my fault! Believe me, little squirrel, it's all Lampwick's fault!"

"And who is this Lampwick?"

"One of my schoolmates. I wanted to go home! I wanted to be obedient! I wanted to study and be a good boy! But Lampwick said to me, 'Why should you bother yourself with studying? Why should you go to school? Come to Playland with us instead — we won't have to learn there. We'll amuse ourselves from morning to night, and we'll always be happy.'"

"And why did you follow the advice of that false friend — of that bad companion?"

"Why? Because, my dear little squirrel, I'm a puppet with no sense, and no heart. Oh, if I only had the least heart, I would never have left that good fairy who loved me like a mother and did so much for me! And I would no longer be a puppet, for by this time I would have become a boy! But if I meet Lampwick, he'll hear what I think of him!"

And he turned to leave. But when he reached the door, he remembered his donkey's ears, and feeling ashamed to show them in public, he took a big cotton cap, put it on his head, and pulled it down to his nose.

He looked everywhere for Lampwick. He looked for him in the streets, in the squares, in the little theatres, in every possible place, but he could not find him. He asked everybody he met, but no one had seen him.

At last he went to his house and knocked on the door.

"Who is it?" asked Lampwick.

"Pinocchio!" answered the puppet.

"Wait a moment, and I'll let you in."

After half an hour the door was opened, and Pinocchio saw that his friend Lampwick was also wearing a big cotton cap on his head pulled down to his nose.

Pinocchio felt almost comforted, and thought to himself, "Does Lampwick have the same illness I have? Is he also suffering from donkey fever?"

Pretending not to have noticed, he smiled and asked, "How are you, my dear Lampwick?"

"Very well. As well as a mouse in a block of cheese."

"Do you mean that?"

"Why should I tell you a lie?"

"But why, then, are you wearing that cotton cap pulled over your ears?"

"The doctor ordered me to wear it because I've hurt my knee. And you, dear puppet, why are you wearing that cotton cap pulled down to your nose?"

"The doctor ordered me to wear it because I've hurt my foot."

"Oh, poor Pinocchio!"

"Oh, poor Lampwick!"

A long silence followed, during which the two friends did nothing but look knowingly at each other.

At last the puppet said softly, "Satisfy my curiosity, my dear Lampwick. Have you ever suffered from a disease of the ears?"

"Never! And you?"

"Never! Except that one of my ears was aching this morning."

"Mine, too."

"Yours, too? And which of your ears hurts?"

"Both of them. And you?"

"Both of them. Do you think we have the same illness?"

"I fear so."

"Will you do me a favour, Lampwick?"

"Yes, of course."

"Will you let me see your ears?"

"Why not? But first, my dear Pinocchio, I'd like to see yours."

"No, you must be the first."

"No, my friend. First you, and then I!"

"Well," said the puppet, "let's agree like good friends."

"What to?"

"We'll take off our caps at the same time. Agreed?"

"Agreed."

And Pinocchio began to count in a loud voice, "One! Two! Three!"

At the word "three", they took off their caps and threw them into the air.

And then a scene followed that would seem incredible if it was not true. When Pinocchio and Lampwick discovered that they had both suffered the same misfortune, instead of feeling full of grief or shame, they tried to wag their ears and teased each other until they burst into laughter.

They laughed, and laughed, and laughed. But Lampwick suddenly stopped. He staggered, turned pale, and said to his friend, "Help, help, Pinocchio!"

"What's the matter?"

"I can no longer stand upright!"

"Neither can I!" exclaimed Pinocchio, tottering and beginning to cry.

And while they were talking, they doubled over and began to run around the room on their hands and feet. As they ran, their hands became hoofs, their faces grew into muzzles, and their backs became covered with a grey, hairy coat sprinkled with black.

The worst, most humiliating moment for the wretched boys, was when they felt their tails growing. Overcome with shame and sorrow, they began to weep and lament their fate.

But if only they had kept quiet! Instead of sighs and lamentations, they could only bray like donkeys, and they brayed loudly in unison: "Hee haw! Hee haw!"

At this moment somebody knocked on the door, and a voice on the outside said, "Open the door! I'm the coachman who brought you here. Open at once, or it will be the worse for you!"

{ Chapter 33 }

Pinocchio becomes a trick donkey

When they did not open the door, the little man forced it open with a violent kick. "Well done, boys! You brayed well, and I recognized you by your voices. That's why I am here," he said to Pinocchio and Lampwick.

The two little donkeys became silent as he came into the room, and stood with their heads down, their ears lowered, and their tails between their legs.

At first the little man stroked and patted them. Then, he combed them until they shone like mirrors. He put halters around their necks and led them to the marketplace in the hope of selling them and making a good profit.

The little man found plenty of buyers. Lampwick was bought by a peasant whose donkey had died the day before. Pinocchio was sold to the director of a company of clowns and tightrope walkers, who intended to teach him to leap and dance with the other animals in the company.

The wicked little man, whose face had seemed so sweet and innocent, made regular journeys around the world with his stagecoach, collecting all the idle children who had taken a dislike to books and school. As soon as his coach was full, he took them to Playland so that they could pass their time playing games. And when, from continual play and no study, these poor, deluded children had become little donkeys, the man packed them off to fairs and markets to be sold. In just a few years, he became a rich man.

What became of Lampwick, I don't know, but from the very first day, Pinocchio had a very hard life.

When he was put into his stall, his master filled the manger with straw, but Pinocchio, having tried a mouthful, spat it out.

Then his master grudgingly filled the manger with hay, but Pinocchio didn't like the hay either.

"So!" exclaimed his master. "Hay does not please you either? Leave it to me, my fussy donkey. I'll find a way to cure you!"

With that, he whipped Pinocchio's legs.

Pinocchio began to cry and brayed, "Hee-haw! I can't digest straw!"

"Then eat hay!" said his master, who understood donkey dialect perfectly.

"Hee-haw! Hay gives me a pain in my stomach."

"Do you mean to tell me that a little donkey like you must be fed chicken breasts and other fine foods?" asked the master, getting more and more angry, and whipping him again.

At this second whipping, Pinocchio held his tongue and said nothing more.

The stable was then shut, and Pinocchio was left alone. He had not eaten for hours, and he began to yawn from hunger. When he yawned, his mouth seemed as wide as an oven.

At last, finding nothing else in the manger, he resigned himself to eating some hay. After he chewed it well, he shut his eyes and swallowed it.

"This hay is not bad," he said to himself, "but it would have been much better if I had gone on with my studies! Instead of hay I might now be eating a loaf of fresh bread and a fine slice of sausage. But I must have patience!"

When he woke up the next morning, he looked in the manger for some more hay, but there was none — he had eaten all night long.

So he took a mouthful of chopped straw. But while he was chewing it, he could not help thinking that the taste of chopped straw was nothing like a tasty plate of macaroni or rice.

"I must be patient!" he repeated as he went on chewing. "Perhaps my example will at least serve as a warning to all disobedient children who don't want to study. Patience! Patience!"

"Patience indeed!" shouted his master, coming into the stable. "Do you think, my little donkey, that I bought you only to give you food and drink? I bought you to make you work so that you might earn money for me. Get up, now! Come with me into the ring, and I'll teach you to jump through hoops, to break through paper frames with your head, to dance waltzes and polkas, and to stand upright on your hind legs."

One way or another, poor Pinocchio had to learn all these tricks. But it was three months before he had learned them, and he received many vicious whippings along the way.

At last the day came when his master was able to announce an extraordinary performance and posters were stuck on street corners throughout the town.

On that evening, the theatre was full an hour before the performance was to begin.

There was not a place to be had either in the pit, the stalls, or the boxes.

The benches around the ring were crowded with children who were curious to see Pinocchio, the famous little donkey, dance.

When the first part of the performance was over, the ringmaster, dressed in a black coat, white shorts, and big leather boots that came above his knees, introduced himself to the audience Making a deep bow, he recited his ridiculous speech. "Respectable public, ladies and gentlemen! The humble undersigned, as a passerby in this illustrious city, I wish to have the honour, not to say the pleasure, of presenting to this intelligent and distinguished audience

GRAND FULL-DRESS PERFORMANCE
TONIGHT
THE USUAL DARING FEATS
AND ASTONISHING PERFORMANCES
BY
ALL THE ARTISTS
AND BY ALL THE HORSES OF THE COMPANY

IN ADDITION
THE FIRST APPEARANCE OF THE FAMOUS
LITTLE DONKEY
PINOCCHIO

CALLED
THE STAR OF THE DANCE
THE THEATRE WILL BE BRILLIANTLY ILLUMINATED

a celebrated little donkey, who has already had the honour of dancing in the presence of the crowned heads of Europe. And thanking you for your attention, I beg of you to help us with your inspiring presence and to forgive us our shortcomings."

The audience laughed and clapped at his speech, but the clapping became even louder when the little donkey Pinocchio appeared in the middle of the ring. He was decked out for the occasion, wearing a new polished leather bridle with brass buckles and studs, and two white flowers in his ears. His mane was divided and curled, and each curl was tied with brightly-coloured bows. He had a gold and silver girth around his body, and his tail was pleated with red and blue velvet ribbons. He was a lovely little donkey!

The ringmaster presented him to the crowd, and said, "My respectable audience! I am not here to tell you tall tales about the great difficulties that I had in capturing and subduing this mammal while he was grazing, wild and free, among the mountains in the plains of the torrid zone. Observe the wild rolling of his eyes. Having tried, in vain, every gentle means to tame him and to accustom him to the life of domestic animals, I was often forced to whip him. But all my goodness to him, instead of gaining his affections, has increased his viciousness. However, following the system of Gall, I discovered in his cranium a bony cartilage, which the Faculty of Medicine in Paris has recognized as the generator of hair, and of dance. Therefore, I have taught him not only to dance, but also to jump through hoops and frames covered with paper. Admire him, and then pass your judgment on him! But before taking my leave of you, permit me, ladies and gentlemen, to invite you to the daily performance that will take place tomorrow evening. In the unfortunate event that the weather should threaten rain, the performance will be moved to tomorrow morning at eleven o'clock."

Here the ringmaster made another deep bow, and then, turning to Pinocchio, said, "Courage, Pinocchio! Before you begin your performance, bow to this distinguished audience – ladies, gentlemen, and children."

Pinocchio obeyed and bent both knees until they touched the ground.

He remained kneeling until the ringmaster cracked his whip and shouted, "Walk!"

Then the little donkey got up and began walking around the ring, keeping perfect step.

After a short while, the ringmaster cried, "Trot!" And Pinocchio trotted.

"Gallop!"

And Pinocchio broke into a gallop.

"Full gallop!"

And Pinocchio ran as fast as he could. Suddenly, while the little donkey was going full speed, the ringmaster rose his arm in the air and fired a pistol.

At the shot, Pinocchio, pretending to be wounded, fell to the ground as if he were really dying.

As he got up from the ground, while the audience clapped and shouted, he looked up and saw a beautiful lady in one of the boxes. Around her neck she wore a medallion on a thick gold chain, and on the medallion was the portrait of a puppet.

"That's my portrait! That's the fairy!" said Pinocchio to himself, recognizing her immediately. He was so overcome with delight that he tried to cry, "Oh, my little fairy! Oh, my dear fairy!"

But instead of these words, a bray came from his throat, so loud and prolonged that the audience roared with laughter, especially the children.

To teach him a lesson, and to make him understand that it is bad manners to bray before the public, the ringmaster hit Pinocchio on the nose with the handle of his whip.

The poor little donkey stuck his tongue out and licked his nose for at least five minutes to ease the pain.

When Pinocchio looked up a second time, he saw that the box was empty. The fairy had disappeared!

He thought he was going to die. His eyes filled with tears, and he began to cry. But nobody noticed, least of all the ringmaster, who, cracking his whip, shouted, "Courage, Pinocchio! Now let the audience see how gracefully you can jump through the hoops."

Pinocchio tried two or three times, but each time he came to the hoop, instead of going through it, he found it easier to go under it. At last he made a leap and went through, but his right leg caught in the hoop, and he fell in a heap on the other side.

When he got up he was lame, and it was only with great difficulty that he managed to return to the stable.

"Bring out Pinocchio! We want the little donkey! Bring out the little donkey!" shouted all the children in the theatre, disappointed by the sad accident.

But the little donkey was not seen again that evening.

The following morning the veterinarian came and declared that Pinocchio would be lame for life.

The director of the company then said to the stable boy, "What do you suppose I can do with a lame donkey? He would eat food without earning it. Take him to the market and sell him."

When they reached the market, a buyer was found at once. He asked the stable boy, "How much do you want for that lame donkey?"

"Five pounds."

"I'll give you five pennies. I'm buying him only for his skin. I can see that it is very hard, and I intend to make a drum with it for the village band."

As soon as the buyer had paid his five pennies, he led the little donkey to the seashore. He put a stone around his neck and tied a long rope around his leg and held on to the end of the rope. The buyer then gave him a sudden push, and Pinocchio was thrown into the water.

Weighed down by the stone, Pinocchio sank straight to the bottom. His owner, keeping a tight hold on the rope, sat down on a rock to wait until the little donkey had drowned, intending then to skin him.

{ *Chapter 34* }

Pinocchio is swallowed by the terrible shark

fter Pinocchio had been underwater for almost an hour, his buyer said to himself, "My poor little lame donkey must be drowned by now. I'll pull him out of the water, and then make a drum with his skin."

He began to pull in the rope that he had tied to the donkey's leg. He pulled, and pulled, and pulled, until at last, instead of a dead donkey, the man saw a live puppet, wriggling like an eel!

When he saw the wooden puppet, the poor man thought he was dreaming. He said nothing and just stood with his mouth open and his eyes bulging out of his head.

Regaining some composure, he asked in a trembling voice, "And the little donkey that I threw into the sea? What's happened to him?"

"I am the little donkey!" said Pinocchio, laughing.

"You?"

"Me!"

"Don't play any tricks on me, you young scamp!"

"Play tricks on you? My dear master, I'm telling the truth."

"But how can you, who were a little donkey just hours ago, have become a wooden puppet?"

"It must have been the effects of seawater. The sea can do extraordinary things."

"Be careful, puppet! Don't think that you can amuse yourself at my expense. You will be in trouble if I lose patience!"

"Well, master, do you want to know the truth? If you free my leg from this rope, I'll tell it to you."

The man, curious to hear the true story, immediately untied the knot, and Pinocchio began to tell his story.

"I was once a puppet as I am now, and I was on the point of becoming a real boy, like so many others. But instead, because I didn't like to study, and because I listened to the advice of bad companions, I ran away from home. And one day when I woke up, I had changed into a donkey with long ears and a long tail! It was such a disgrace! I was taken to the market and sold to the director of a circus company, who decided to make a famous dancer of me, and a famous leaper through hoops. But one night, during a performance, I had a bad fall in the ring that made me lame, so the director, not knowing what to do with a lame donkey, sent me to be sold, and you bought me!"

"That is only too true! I paid five pennies for you. Now who will give me back my money?"

"And why did you buy me? You bought me to make a drum with! A drum!"

"That's true! And now where will I find another skin?"

"Don't despair, master. There are so many little donkeys in the world!"

"Tell me, you impertinent rascal, does your story end here?"

"No," answered the puppet. "I have a few more words to say, and then I'll have finished. After you bought me, you brought me here to kill me. But you preferred to tie a stone around my neck and throw me into the sea to drown. I'll always be grateful to you for this humane sentiment. Nevertheless, dear master, you made your plans without considering the fairy!"

"Who is this fairy?"

"She is my mother, and is like all good mothers who care for their children and never lose sight of them, and help them when they deserve to be abandoned. Well, the good fairy, as soon as she saw that I was in danger of drowning, sent a huge shoal of fish, who thought I really was a little dead donkey, and began to eat me. I would never have thought that fish were greedier than boys! Some ate my ears, some my muzzle, others my neck and mane, some the skin of my legs, and some my coat. Among them was a little fish so polite that he even condescended to eat my tail."

"I swear that I'll never eat fish again," said the horrified buyer. "It would be too dreadful to open a mullet, or a fried whiting, and find a donkey's tail inside!"

"I agree with you," said the puppet, laughing. "When the fish had finished eating the donkey's hide that covered me from head to foot, they reached the bone, or rather, the wood — I am made of the hardest wood. But after taking a few bites, they soon discovered that I was too hard for their teeth. Disgusted with such indigestible food, some went off in one direction, and some in another, without even saying 'thank you'. And now at last I've told you how it came to be that when you pulled up the rope you found a live puppet instead of a dead donkey."

"Enough of your story!" cried the man angrily. "I paid five pennies for you, and I want my money back! Do you know what I'll do? I'll take you back to the market and sell you for firewood!"

"Sell me if you like. It makes no difference to me," said Pinocchio.

But as he said this, he jumped back into the water and, swimming happily away from the shore, called to his poor owner, "Goodbye, master! The next time you want a skin to make a drum, remember me!" And he laughed and went on swimming.

After a while he turned again and shouted louder, "Goodbye, master! The next time you want a little well-seasoned firewood, remember me!"

Soon he had swum so far that he was barely visible. All that could be seen of him was a little black speck on the surface of the sea that from time to time lifted its legs out of the water and leaped and tumbled like a joyful dolphin.

Pinocchio was swimming along feeling relaxed and carefree, when he saw a rock in the middle of the sea that looked as if it was made of white marble. On top stood a beautiful little goat, who bleated lovingly and beckoned Pinocchio towards it.

But the most peculiar thing was this: the little goat's hair, instead of being white or black, or a mixture of two colours, as is usual with goats, was blue, and a very vivid blue, very much like the hair of the beautiful child.

Pinocchio swam as fast as he could towards the white rock. He was already halfway there when he saw the horrible head of a sea monster, rising up out of the water and rushing towards him. Its open, cavernous mouth and three rows of enormous teeth would have been terrifying to look at even in a picture.

This sea monster was the gigantic shark who has been mentioned more than once in this story, and who, for its horrible killings and insatiable appetite, was called the "Attila of fish and fishermen."

Pinocchio was terrified. He tried to avoid the monster, but that huge, gaping mouth came towards him as quickly as an arrow.

"Hurry, Pinocchio, hurry!" bleated the beautiful little goat.

Pinocchio swam desperately, using all his strength.

"Quick, Pinocchio, the monster is close behind you!"

Pinocchio swam quicker than ever, flying like a bullet from a gun. He had nearly reached the rock, and the little goat had stretched out her forelegs to help him out of the water . . .

But it was too late! The monster caught him and, drawing in its breath, sucked the poor puppet into its mouth. It swallowed with such violence that Pinocchio was knocked unconscious for a quarter of an hour, as he fell into the shark's stomach.

When he came to, he had no idea where he was. It was very dark all around him, and the darkness was so deep that it seemed to him that he had fallen headfirst into a bottle of ink. He listened, but he could hear nothing except for the great gusts of wind that blew in his face from time to time. At first, he did not know where the wind came from, but at last he discovered that it came from the monster's lungs — for the shark suffered from asthma. When it breathed, it was exactly as if a north wind was blowing.

Pinocchio tried to be brave, but when he was certain that he was trapped in the shark's body, he began to cry and scream and call out, "Help! Help! Oh, poor me! Will nobody come to save me?"

"Who do you think could save you, you unhappy wretch?" said a voice in the dark that sounded like an out-of-tune guitar.

"Who's there?" asked Pinocchio, frozen with terror.

"It is me – a poor tuna fish who was swallowed by the shark at the same time you were. And what kind of fish are you?"

"I am not a fish. I'm a puppet."

"If you're not a fish, why did you let yourself be swallowed by the monster?"

"I didn't let myself be swallowed. The monster swallowed me! And now what are we to do here in the dark?"

"Resign ourselves and wait until the shark has digested us."

"But I don't want to be digested!" howled Pinocchio, beginning to cry again.

"Neither do I," added the tuna fish, "but I'm wise enough to think that when one is born a tuna fish, it's more dignified to die in the water than in oil."

"Nonsense!" cried Pinocchio.

"That's my opinion," replied the tuna fish, "and opinions ought to be respected."

"Nevertheless, I want to get away from here. I want to escape!"

"Escape then, if you can!"

"Is this shark who has swallowed us very big?" asked the puppet.

"Big? His body is a mile long, not counting his tail."

While they were talking, in the pitch dark, Pinocchio thought he saw a light a long way off.

"What's that little light I see in the distance?" he asked.

"It's most likely some companion in misfortune who, like us, is waiting to be digested."

"I will go and find him. Do you think it may be some old fish who could perhaps show us how to escape?"

"I hope so, dear puppet."

"Goodbye, tuna fish."

"Goodbye, puppet, and good luck!"

"Where will we meet again?"

"Who knows? It's better not to think of it."

{ *Chapter 35* }

Father and son together again

Having said goodbye to the tuna fish, Pinocchio began to grope his way through the dark body of the shark, taking one step at a time in the direction of the dim light he saw shining at a great distance.

The further he went, the brighter the light became. He walked and walked, until at last he reached it. And when he reached it, he found a little table with a lighted candle, stuck into a green glass bottle on it. And seated at the table was a little old man. He was eating some fish, and they were so much alive that they sometimes even jumped out of his mouth while he was eating them.

Seeing the old man, Pinocchio was filled with such great and unexpected joy that he became almost delirious. He wanted to laugh, to cry, and to say a thousand things, but he could only stammer out a few confused and broken words. Finally he succeeded in uttering a cry of joy and, throwing his arms around the little old man's neck, began to shout, "Oh, my dear father! I've found you at last! I'll never leave you again — never, never, never!"

"Do my eyes tell me the truth?" said the little old man, rubbing his eyes. "Are you really my dear Pinocchio?"

"Yes, yes, I really am Pinocchio! Have you forgiven me? Oh, my dear father, how

good you are! To think that I . . . Oh! But if you only knew what bad luck I have had and everything that has happened to me! The day that you sold your coat to buy me a spelling book so that I could go to school, I went to see the puppet show, and the Showman wanted to throw me on the fire so that he could finish roasting a sheep. And he was the same man who later gave me five gold pieces to take to you, but I met the fox and the cat, and they took me to the Lobster Inn, where they ate like wolves. I left by myself in the middle of the night and came across two assassins. They chased me – I ran and ran, and they still followed me, and I ran, until they hung me from a branch of a tree called the Big Oak. Then the beautiful child with blue hair sent a little carriage to fetch me. When the doctors saw me, they said, 'If he is not dead, it's proof that he is still alive.' And then I told a lie, and my nose began to grow until I could no longer get through the door of the room, so I went with the fox and the cat to bury the four gold pieces – I had already spent one at the inn – and the parrot began to laugh, and instead of two thousand gold pieces, there were none. When he heard that I had been robbed, the judge had me thrown into prison. Then, when I left the prison, I saw a bunch of grapes in a field, and I was caught in a trap, and the peasant, who had every right, put a dog collar around my neck to make me guard the chicken yard. Later he accepted my innocence and he let me go. Then the serpent with the smoking tail began to laugh and broke a blood vessel. And so I returned to the house of the beautiful child, who was dead, and the pigeon, seeing that I was crying, said, 'I have seen your father. He was building a little boat to go and look for you.' And I said to him, 'Oh! If only I had wings,' and he said to me, 'Do you want to go to your father?' and I said, 'Yes, but who will take me to him?' and he said, 'I'll take you,' and I said, 'How?' and he said, 'Get on my back.' And so we flew all night, and in the morning, all the fishermen who were looking out to sea said, 'There is a poor man in a boat who is on the verge of being drowned', and I recognized you at once, even at that distance, and I signalled to you to return to land."

"I recognized you, too," said Geppetto, "and I would have returned to the shore, but I couldn't! The sea was furious, and a huge wave capsized my boat. Then this monstrous shark saw me in the water, took hold of me with its tongue, and swallowed me as if I had been a cake."

"How long have you been here?" asked Pinocchio.

"Since that day. It must be nearly two years ago. Two years, my dear Pinocchio, that have seemed like two centuries!"

"And how have you managed to live? Where did you get the candle? And the matches? Who gave them to you?"

"Stop, and I'll tell you everything. During that same storm in which my boat was overturned, a merchant ship was heavily damaged. The sailors were all saved, but the ship sank to the bottom, and the shark, who was particularly hungry that day, swallowed the whole ship."

"How?"

"He swallowed it in one mouthful, and the only thing he spat out was the mainmast, which stuck between his teeth like a fish bone. Fortunately for me, the ship was full of tinned meat, biscuits, bottles of wine, dried raisins, cheese, coffee, sugar, candles, and boxes of wax matches. I've been able to live on these provisions for two years. But now there's nothing left, and this candle is the last one."

"And after that?"

"After that, dear boy, everything will be dark again."

"There's no time to lose, Father." said Pinocchio. "We must escape."

"Escape? But how?"

"We could escape through the shark's mouth, throw ourselves into the sea, and swim away."

"That's all very well, Pinocchio, but I don't know how to swim."

"That doesn't matter, I'm a good swimmer. You can get on my back, and I'll carry you safely to shore."

"It's no use, my boy," replied Geppetto, shaking his head with a sad smile. "A puppet like you, barely three feet tall, would not have the strength to swim with me on his back."

"Try it and see!"

Without another word, Pinocchio took the candle in his hand and said to his father, "Follow me, and don't be afraid."

So they walked for some time and crossed the body and the stomach of the shark. But when they arrived at the monster's throat, they thought it better to stop, look around, and choose the best moment to escape.

The shark was very old, it suffered from asthma and a weak heart, and had to sleep with its mouth open. So when Pinocchio approached the monster's throat and looked up he saw a large strip of starry sky and beautiful moonlight beyond the enormous gaping mouth.

"This is it," he whispered to his father. "The shark is sleeping like a mouse, the sea is calm, and it's as light as day. Follow me, dear Father, and we'll soon be free!"

They climbed up the throat of the monster, and when they reached its enormous mouth, they began to tiptoe down its tongue.

Before taking the final leap, the puppet said to his father, "Get on my back and put your arms around my neck. I'll take care of the rest."

As soon as Geppetto was firmly settled on his son's back, Pinocchio threw himself into the water and began to swim. The sea was smooth as oil, the moon shone brilliantly, and the shark was sleeping so soundly that even cannon fire would not have woken it.

{ Chapter 36 }

At last Pinocchio becomes a real boy

hile Pinocchio was swimming towards the shore, he realized that his father was trembling as violently as if he had a fever.

Was he trembling from cold or from fear? Perhaps a little of both. But, thinking that it was from fear, Pinocchio said, "Be brave, Father! In a few minutes we'll be safely on shore."

"But where is the shore?" asked the little old man, becoming still more frightened, and squinting his eyes as tailors do when they want to thread a needle. "I've been looking in every direction, and I see nothing but the sky and the sea."

"I can see the shore quite well," said the puppet. "You must know that I'm like a cat. I see better by night than by day."

Poor Pinocchio was pretending to be in good spirits, but in fact he was beginning to worry. He was exhausted and was gasping and panting for breath, and the shore was still a long way off.

He swam until he had no breath left. Then he turned to Geppetto and said, "Father, help me! I'm dying!"

Father and son were on the verge of drowning when they heard a voice like an out- of-tune guitar, "Who is dying?"

"It is me, and my poor father!"

"I know that voice! You're Pinocchio!"

"Yes! And who are you?"

"I am the tuna fish, your prison companion in the shark."

"How did you manage to escape?"

"I followed your example. You showed me the way, and I escaped after you."

"Tuna fish, you've arrived just in time! Please help us."

"Of course, with pleasure! Take hold of my tail, and leave the rest to me. You will reach the shore in four minutes."

Geppetto and Pinocchio accepted the offer at once. But instead of grabbing hold of the fish's tail, they thought it would be more comfortable to ride on the tuna's back.

Once they reached the shore, Pinocchio sprang onto the beach first and then helped his father. He turned to the tuna fish and said, "My friend, you have saved my father's life. I cannot find the right words to thank you properly. Let me at least give you a kiss as a sign of my gratitude!"

The tuna fish raised his head out of the water, and Pinocchio kissed him tenderly between the eyes. At this spontaneous show of affection, the poor tuna, who was not used to it, was extremely moved and, not wanting to be seen crying like a child, dived under the water and disappeared.

Meanwhile, day had dawned. Pinocchio offered his arm to Geppetto, who could barely stand, and said, "Lean on my arm, dear Father, and let's go. We'll walk very slowly, like the ants, and when we're tired, we can rest."

"And where will we go?" asked Geppetto.

"In search of some house or cottage where they will give us a little food and some straw to sleep on."

They had not gone far when they saw two villainous-looking individuals begging at the roadside.

They were the cat and the fox, but they were barely recognizable. The cat had pretended to be blind for so long that she really had become blind. And the fox was old and mangy, paralyzed down one side, and he had lost his tail. Having fallen on very hard times, the fox found himself obliged to sell his beautiful tail to a travelling pedlar, who bought it to drive away flies.

"Oh, Pinocchio!" cried the fox. "Give a little charity to two poor invalids!"

"Invalids!" repeated the cat.

"Go away, impostors!" answered the puppet. "You cheated me once, but you will never cheat me again."

"Believe me, Pinocchio, we are now truly poor and miserable!"

"Poor and miserable!" repeated the cat.

"If you're poor and miserable, you deserve it. Remember the proverb: 'Stolen money never bears fruit.' Goodbye, impostors!"

"Have pity on us!"

"On us!"

"Goodbye, impostors! Remember the proverb: 'He who steals his neighbour's cloak ends his life without a shirt!'"

On saying this, Pinocchio and Geppetto went on their way. A little further on, they saw a little brick and tile cottage, with a straw roof.

"Someone must live there," said Pinocchio. "Let's go and knock at the door."

They went and knocked.

"Who's there?" said a little voice from inside.

"We are a poor father and son without bread and with nowhere to go," answered the puppet.

"Turn the key, and the door will open," said the same little voice.

Pinocchio turned the key, and the door opened. They went in and looked everywhere, but they could see no one.

"Hello! Is there anyone here?" said Pinocchio.

"Here I am, up here!"

They looked up to the ceiling, and there on a beam was the talking grasshopper.

"Oh, my dear little grasshopper!" said Pinocchio, bowing politely to him.

"Ah! Now you call me your 'dear little grasshopper'. But do you remember the time when you threw a mallet at me, to drive me from your house?"

"You're right, grasshopper! Drive me away, too! Throw a mallet at me, but have pity on my poor father."

"I'll have pity on both of you, but I wanted to remind you of your cruelty, to teach you that, when it is possible, we should be kind to everybody, if we want others to be kind to us in our hour of need."

"You're right, you're right, and I'll remember this lesson. But tell me, how did you manage to buy this beautiful hut?"

"This hut was given to me yesterday by a goat whose wool was a beautiful blue colour."

"And where has the goat gone?" asked Pinocchio.

"I don't know."

"When will it come back?"

"It will never come back. It went away yesterday, bleating in great grief as if to say, 'Poor Pinocchio. I'll never see him again. By this time, he must have been devoured by the shark!'"

"Did it really say that? Then it was her! It was my dear little fairy," exclaimed Pinocchio, sobbing bitterly.

Pinocchio dried his eyes and made up a comfortable straw bed for Geppetto. Then he asked the grasshopper, "Tell me, where might I find a glass of milk for my father?"

"A gardener called Giangio keeps cows three fields away from here. Go to him, and you might get some milk."

Pinocchio ran all the way to Giangio's house. Once there, the gardener asked him, "How much milk do you want?"

"A glassful."

"A glass of milk costs a penny. Where is your money?"

"I don't have any," replied Pinocchio, quite saddened.

"That's too bad," answered the gardener. "If you have no money for me, I have no milk for you."

"Patience!" said Pinocchio, and he turned to go.

"Wait a minute," said Giangio. "Perhaps we can manage something. Can you work a pumping machine?"

"What's a pumping machine?"

"It's a machine that draws up water from the well to water the vegetables."

"I can try."

"If you draw a hundred buckets of water, I'll give you a glass of milk."

"It's a deal!"

Giangio led Pinocchio to the garden and taught him to operate the pumping machine. Pinocchio set to work immediately, but before he had drawn up the hundred buckets of water, the sweat was pouring from his head to his feet.

He had never worked so hard.

"Up until now," said the gardener, "my little donkey turned the pumping machine.
But the poor animal is dying."

"May I go and see him?" said Pinocchio.

"Of course."

When Pinocchio went into the stable, he saw a little donkey stretched out on the
straw, worn out from hunger and overwork. After looking at him carefully, he said to

himself, "I'm sure I know this little donkey! His face is very familiar." He bent over him and asked in donkey language, "Who are you?"

At this question the little donkey opened his dying eyes and answered, "I . . . am . . . Lamp . . . wick."

Then, closing his eyes again, he died.

"Oh, poor Lampwick!" said Pinocchio in a low voice, as he dried a tear that was rolling down his face.

"Why do you grieve for a donkey that cost you nothing?" said the gardener. "I paid good money for him! Now what will I do?"

"He was my friend!"

"Your friend?"

"One of my schoolmates!"

"What?" shouted Giangio, laughing loudly. "You had donkeys for schoolmates? I can only imagine what wonderful lessons you must have had!"

The puppet, who felt very ashamed by these words, did not answer, but took his glass of milk and returned to the hut.

From that day, for more than five months, he got up at dawn every morning to go and work the pumping machine, to earn a glass of milk for his father. But that wasn't all he did. During his spare time, he learned to make woven baskets, and with the money he made by selling them, he was able to pay for everything they needed. He also built an elegant little wheelchair, in which he could take his father out for fresh air when the weather was fine.

Not only did Pinocchio look after his father, but he also managed to save forty pennies to buy himself a new coat.

One morning he said to his father, "I'm going to the market to buy a jacket, a cap, and a pair of shoes. When I return," he added, laughing, "I'll be so well-dressed that you'll mistake me for a fine gentleman."

After leaving the house, he began to run merrily and happily along. Suddenly, he heard someone call his name. He turned around and saw a big snail crawling out from the hedge.

"Don't you know me?" asked the snail.

"Perhaps, but I'm not sure."

"Don't you remember the snail who served the fairy with blue hair? Don't you remember the time when I came downstairs to let you in, and you were caught by your foot, which you had stuck through the front door?"

"I remember it all," shouted Pinocchio. "Tell me quickly, my beautiful little snail, where have you left my good fairy? What is she doing? Has she forgiven me? Does she still remember me? Does she still love me? Is she far from here? Can I go and see her?"

The snail replied with her usual slowness, "My dear Pinocchio, the poor fairy is lying in bed at the hospital!"

"At the hospital?"

"Yes. Many bad things have happened to her and she has become very ill. She doesn't even have enough money to buy herself a mouthful of bread."

"Is it true? Oh, what terrible news you have given me! Oh, poor fairy! Poor, poor fairy! If I had a million pounds, I would carry them to her immediately! But I have only forty pennies. With them I was going to buy a new coat. But take them, snail, and carry them at once to my good fairy."

"And your new coat?"

"What does a new coat matter? I would even sell these rags I have on if it would help her. Go, snail, and be quick; and come back here in two days, for I hope I'll be able to give you some more money then. Until now, I've worked to look after my father. From now on, I'll work another five hours each day so that I may also take care of my good mother. Goodbye, snail! I'll expect you in two days!"

The snail, most surprisingly, began to run like a lizard under the hot August sun.

That evening, instead of going to bed at ten o'clock, Pinocchio sat up 'til midnight, and instead of making eight baskets, he made sixteen.

Then he went to bed and fell asleep. And while he slept, he thought he saw the fairy, smiling and beautiful, who kissed him and said, "Well done, Pinocchio! To reward you for your good heart, I'll forgive you for all your past misdeeds. Boys who take care of their parents, and help them when they are poor and sick, deserve great praise and love, even if they are not models of obedience and good behaviour. Try and do better in the future, and you'll be happy."

Then the dream ended, and Pinocchio woke up.

He was astonished when he discovered that he was no longer a wooden puppet, but a boy, a boy like all other boys! He looked around and saw that the straw roof of the hut had disappeared. He was in a pretty little room that was simply but elegantly furnished. Jumping out of bed, he found a new suit of clothes ready for him, a new cap, and a pair of new leather boots that fitted him beautifully.

When he was dressed, he put his hands in his pockets and pulled out a little ivory purse on which it said: "The blue-haired fairy returns the forty pennies to her dear Pinocchio, and thanks him for his good heart". He opened the purse, and instead of forty copper pennies, he found forty shining gold pieces.

He then went and looked at himself in the mirror, and he thought he was someone else. For he no longer saw the usual reflection of a wooden puppet. He saw instead the reflection of a bright, intelligent boy with chestnut hair and blue eyes, looking contented and happy.

Pinocchio felt quite bewildered, and he could not tell if he was awake or dreaming with his eyes open.

"Where is my father?" he exclaimed suddenly, and going into the next room, he found old Geppetto quite well, lively, and in good spirits, just as he had been years ago. He had already taken up his wood-carving again, and he was designing a rich and beautiful frame of leaves, flowers, and animal heads.

"Tell me, dear Father," said Pinocchio, throwing his arms around his neck and kissing him. "How can this sudden change be explained?"

"This sudden change is all your doing," answered Geppetto.

"How is it my doing?"

"Because when children who have been naughty turn over a new leaf and become good, they have the power to bring happiness to their families."

"And the old wooden Pinocchio, where is he?"

"There he is," answered Geppetto, and he pointed to a big puppet leaning against a chair, its head on one side, its arms dangling, and its legs so crossed and bent that it was really a miracle that it remained standing.

Pinocchio turned and looked at it for a moment, and then said happily to himself, "How ridiculous I was when I was a puppet! I am so glad to be a real boy at last!"

The End